WE CAN'T ALL BE ANGELS

WE CAN'T ALL BE ANGELS

Steve Barret

The Book Guild Ltd
Sussex, England

This book is a work of fiction. The characters and situations in this story are imaginary. No resemblance is intended between these characters and any real persons, either living or dead.

The Book Guild Ltd.
25 High Street,
Lewes, Sussex

First published 1997

Set in Baskerville
Typesetting by Raven Typesetters, Chester
Printed in Great Britain by
Bookcraft (Bath) Ltd, Avon

A catalogue record for this book is
available from the British Library

ISBN 1 85776 178 2

To Arlette

In memory of Anna and Auguste.

Special thanks to Peter Burgess, Leslie Abbott, Daniel Bonnier and Bernard Prolat.

'If God exists, that is Her problem.'

(Painted on the Sorbonne wall, Paris, May 1968)

1

Desperately, Bob Treillet struggled to understand what was happening to him.

His body, or perhaps it was his soul, was moving fast along a tunnel of some kind, a silent tube with fleshy walls. He might almost have been travelling through his own intestine.

That much, at least, he managed to register. But why was everything so gloomy? Why was he suffocating in this dim red glow? Why was he so afraid?

Now past forty, he should have learned to control crises well enough, but this was something quite new, and he couldn't handle it.

Explanations came and went, like someone zapping on TV. And eventually he knew he'd had an accident of some kind. Someone had let him down. He was starting to work it out. If he'd had an accident, he must be in a hospital somewhere. He must be in a coma being operated on. Think, think, think. He lived on the edge of Saint-Tropez, in France. He was French. That much was true.

Everything went black and a new thought pattern began. An insidious question perturbed the ebb and flow of his thoughts. Submerged in the tidal wave of uncertainties great enough to mystify the Pope himself was the riddle: who was responsible for his accident? Sabotage. His alter ego, whom he fondly called his Other Self, played a dirty trick on him. That was it, his impulsive vivacious side had been held back again by his Other Self, a mean sort of a conscience that was always telling him that disaster lay ahead.

Whew! He had identified the adversary, solved that part of the mystery. And now he was rushing headlong into – what?

The gloom in the tunnel seemed to lessen, and he began to relish his little victory. At any rate he could still reason things out.

Something long and slimy was wrapping itself round one of his wrists. A new terror gripped him as he recognized the thing: a snake! He had a horror of snakes, rats and anything else of a creepy nature.

Treillet shook the snake off, only to find that he was being escorted along by other horrors, strange evil-looking creatures that shone in the dark. Monsters from the bowels of the earth, or from hell. Nom de Dieu! perhaps he was in Hell!

No, that couldn't be right. You had to go before your Maker first of all, be judged, sent to Purgatory or Limbo. And if it were Purgatory, it meant he would eventually reach Heaven.

Again he was breathing easier, engaging in rational thought and relieved to know it.

The red glow was even brighter now, paler, and unless he was mistaken that was a flashing beacon of some sort farther along the tunnel.

New anguish seized him. He became aware of a muffled bell tolling. There was a jolt and he sprawled full length, his face landing in a gooey stinking mess. An alligator was splashing through the muck to attack him, its jaws open wide. He tried to scream but no sound came out. Treillet hurled himself to one side and lay gulping for air.

This was ridiculous, an alligator of all things. He'd never seen a real alligator in his whole life. He was seeing things, it was all a goddam dream. A nightmare for Pete's sake! All he had to do was concentrate and pinch himself and he would wake up.

He burst out of the tunnel and found himself in a blinding light. Coming to a halt, he stood trembling, utterly perplexed. He tried to pinch himself but his arm wouldn't move.

To his horror, he realized it was not a nightmare. This was for real. Robert Treillet, forty five, composer and pop star known professionally as Bob Treillet and domiciled at Saint-Tropez on the Mediterranean coast, had crashed his ULM flying flea, a motorized French glider. That much was certain.

The initials U.S.C. were marked above a door. He walked slowly to the half open door, making no sound, and went through. Inside he found he was in a room with white walls. Glancing up he saw that there was no ceiling, just a beautiful cloudless blue sky above. On the far wall at waist height he saw an anthracite-coloured computer unit, its keyboard having huge black letters on white tabs that looked like gravestones. A large screen was fixed above the computer. Treillet shivered in the eerie silence.

On that same wall was a mirror, which he approached to examine. He let out a gasp; reflected back at him was a naked body with the texture of a wax doll. His face showed craggy, grey and expressionless. Treillet felt himself frowning but the face in the mirror did not alter. That must mean he was looking death in the face! Yet his mind was still functioning …

It was all too much for him and he wanted to cry. The emotion was present but the tears wouldn't come.

A shape came out of the wall and halted before him. He recoiled. It became a person, a strange man about fifty years of age, slightly overweight and with tiny piggy eyes that twinkled. The apparition was wearing a black tail suit and a shiny red bowler hat. It studied Treillet for a long moment, stroking a long white tunic held over its arm. It then threw the tunic across to Treillet, and nodded. Treillet put the tunic on, hastily concealing his nudity.

The ghost, angel or whatever it was fiddled with his bow tie, adjusted the elastic band affair that held his hair in a pony tail, then doffed his bowler in a flourish of welcome. The fellow had a golden cane and, to Bob's amazement, performed a little tap dance.

'Allow me to introduce myself,' the apparition said in an American accent. 'I'm Archie Mackenzie, originally from Brooklyn, but I spent most of my life in Manhattan. You will note the strains of the well-known number New York, New York now accompanying us. My earthly existence was in fact cut short on a Broadway stage. Big Apple, as it is known in the familiar, possessed my very soul. It was my only real love.' He ended in a throaty diminuendo.

The entry of this vaudeville has-been forced Bob to think again. Perhaps it was a nightmare after all. Weren't dreams a kind of sorting office of the mind? Fortunately events had taken a turn for the better, certainly better than the harrowing experience of the monsters in the tunnel. This Mackenzie chap seemed well disposed towards him. Ha, ha, he'd wake up soon and start laughing. He would describe it all to Bernard and Olga.

'The last voyager we had reached here quite a while back,' the fellow went on. 'I guess you're trying to figure out what's happened to you. You've had a bit of a shock, and you need time to think.'

'I've been trying to.'

Mackenzie gave him a friendly smile and continued in a sing-song voice.

'A voyager, in our sense, is a human being in transit between life and death, and I'm afraid I must ask you to go back where you came from, if you don't mind. Sorry, but I don't make the rules around here. It's tough enough for me to keep them.'

He pointed a long blue-nailed finger at the floor with meaning. Treillet glanced anxiously at the open door as the other gave a languid shrug.

'Naturally, you're worried about those creatures in the tunnel. That's your subconscious playing tricks on you. When I came here they were dressed as undertakers and sang excerpts from Mozart's Requiem. Pretty darned depressing. You've no idea the trouble I had getting the folk here to accept my improvements in the service. I've suggested they set up a reception desk with a cuckoo clock on the wall behind it but they turned it down.'

Mackenzie repeated his tap dance: 'All right, not quite up to Fred Astaire, but it'll pass. He made his name in movies, and he could always do another take if he wasn't satisfied. It's quite different on the stage. Yeah, well let's talk turkey. You have blundered, my friend, into the U.S.C., the Universal Selection Centre, and you were not expected. You must rejoin your body in the hospital and you'll find it'll all pan out fine. Well, there you are.'

'W-What do you mean, there I am? Where am I?'

'I've just told you. Now don't you get smart with me. Just calm down, learn to meditate. Let me tell you a story about meditation. There were these monks in the Tibetan mountains sitting in a circle contemplating. After a while one of the monks pulled up his robe and started unscrewing his navel. He got it out a coupla inches and stopped. And the others said: "Does it come right out?", and he said: "Sure it does" and he screwed it right out. "A miracle," they all cried. He stood up to take a bow, and his ass fell off!'

They both laughed, and Mackenzie added: 'I just love jokes. You just can't get anywhere in show business without jokes.'

'That's for sure.'

The entertainer continued.

'About that mirror, I can see it fascinates you. It's reflecting an imitation of your body, it's made of a special plastic material. If you touch it you won't feel a thing.'

To demonstrate his point Archie gave him a pat on the shoulder. Bob's jaw dropped, he had not felt the gesture.

'The material is one of my inventions,' Archie said. 'As you undoubtedly know, the soul is invisible to the naked eye, an unidentifiable flying object as you might say. So I thought it would be nice for the voyagers in transit when they turn up here to find their old familiar friend, the body. But see here, you'd better get moving, the sky's turning a little grey.'

The Frenchman glanced overhead where the azure blue had changed to a sooty nuance. Black depression took hold of him, he gave a moan and crumpled at Archie's feet, face and arms outstretched.

'Holy shit! Mackenzie snapped. 'What's he playing at now?'

* * *

As he lay prostrate, Treillet's memory flashed back over the life-long tussle he'd had with his Other Self. The conflict was not over by a long shot, now that he was in a state of living death. Schizophrenia had dogged him on and off throughout his life, and it was quite unnecessary if only his Other Self had been willing to adapt to the volatile world of showbiz.

Bob was an artist whose very survival depended on inspiration, intuition and a carefree openness towards his public. He had no use for that other part of himself whose virtues were of caution, rumination and logical reasoning. True, the two personalities had managed to cohabit after a fashion but the result had nearly driven him mad at times. The optimist in him had gained the upper hand as he steadily matured. Alas, now the wet blanket in him had counter-attacked.

That very morning the enemy had tried a new ploy, standing like some evil spirit at the foot of his king size bed and giving him violent spasms akin to epilepsy. Furious at this attack, Bob had snarled at him, then switched tactics and tried to reason with him, stressing that they were both in the same boat as you might say, there could be neither winner nor loser. Much good did it do him, for the Other Self had stepped up the spasms, rocking him and heaving him about in a force ten on the Richter scale. It surprised Bob that an associate with a claim to common sense should seek to compete with him in such capricious behaviour. It was quite out of character, and he feared they were both slipping into mindless idiocy.

More generally the Other Self had upbraided him for aiming at shallow success, urging Bob to concentrate on 'true values in life', whatever they were. He told him that his need for success was 'feckless', it stemmed from his manic depressive temperament, he should grow up and cease grovelling to commercial interests. Bob, whose public image was that of a rebel against The System, had subsequently begun turning out numbers with no punch to them, whereat the Other Self accused him of 'mediocrity' and forecast disaster for him in the demanding pop music jungle, where innovation was vital. Bob told him to make up his bloody mind, and his Other Self gave him an injection of adrenalin that knocked him out with severe migraine for weeks on end.

Finally Treillet, judging that compromise was impossible and that his two selves were caught in a profitless battle of wills, resolved to end the deadlock. He penned a song with the title Death to My Other Half. Not only that, he spread it around that he was an incurable schizophrenic, demanding a court order that he should be taken into care. Treillet reckoned that his enemy would thus be forced to beat a retreat, leaving him in peace to get on with his career. In a fit of righteous anger he dismissed his foe, sending him to the 'outer darkness', as he grandly described it.

The only outcome was that his manager ordered him to take a long rest out of the public eye.

Came the day that Bob invited a few friends, totalling close on 400, to a party at his converted farmhouse outside Saint-Tropez. It was a celebration for his latest hit. The climax of the occasion was a display of his brand new ULM. As he flew the machine over the cottage at little more than tree height, heading for the salmon pink sunset, Treillet felt pretty much like Stravinsky's Firebird in person. He couldn't recall what the bird was actually supposed to have done but he imagined it must have resembled a phoenix rising from the ashes. He had never felt more cheerful.

Bob had by now forgotten his Other Self, who chose that precise moment in time to inflict on him an excruciating toothache that numbed his senses. He lost his sense of height, could no longer gauge his direction with the seat of his pants, and the ULM got out of control. Whatever fire-birds got up to, they didn't have toothache and certainly never flapped their wings like a parrot falling off its perch. Which was exactly how the ULM performed, crunching into a group of nearby rocks while the guests stood with glasses in their hands, openmouthed, aghast and powerless.

And now on the floor of the white-walled room in the Centre, our hero was coming out of his faint and became conscious of the surroundings. He had to admit that the Other Self, camouflaging his dirty trick as an accident, could claim a signal victory. Their war of attrition was still on!

Blinking and sniffling, Bob saw a stern-visaged woman, aged sixty if she were a day, surging through the wall at him. She towered above Treillett, hands on hips. The woman had grey hair held back in a bun and wore a strict black skirt to mid-calf with a stiff white shirt buttoned to the throat. She looked down at him with eyes of steel, the very picture of the history mistress at his junior school.

'What is the matter with him, Archibald?' she demanded. 'We don't allow people to pass out here.' The woman scowled at Mackenzie. 'What have you been doing to him? Answer me, you blithering fool.'

'How should I know why he passed out? I didn't do a thing, honestly boss.'

'I have told you a hundred times, don't call me boss. My name is Lady Daisy.'

'Yes boss - er- Lady Daisy.'

The woman flourished a clipboard and marked a cross on it half way down. She made to shake Treillet but had second thoughts:

'It's a male, ugh. Anyhow, at his age one doesn't faint for no reason. You must have said something frightful.'

Treillet noted that her ladyship had a la-di-da accent, and supposed she was from the English upper crust. She certainly sounded crusty enough, nothing like the Beatles.

'I didn't do anything special, you gotta believe me boss, I mean Daisy.'

'Ridiculous,' she scoffed in a fair imitation of a lady prime minister lecturing a Brussels Eurocrat. 'Don't tell me lies, Archibald. Get him up this minute.'

Archie's face screwed up in a puckish ear-to-ear smile:

'Get him up? Try mouth to mouth resuscitation. Give him a French kiss, that should get him straight up. Who knows, you might like it too.'

'Don't be impertinent. That's your fifth insolent remark today. Give him a slap or two on the face, we've wasted enough time.'

Mackenzie obeyed, slapping Bob on the face to bring him round. His superior scanned the clipboard and read out: 'Robert Treillet, male, age forty five, nationality French, musician, living in Saint-Tropez, a sinkhole of perdition if ever there were one.'

'Sea, sex and sun,' crooned Archie with remembered pleasure.

'Control yourself, Archibald.'

Treillet let out a groan and mumbled: 'What's going on? What a nightmare! I'm sick of it. I want to wake up ...'

'How do you do, Monsieur Treillet? I am Lady Daisy Sniffington-Madley, late of Buckingham Palace. And take that grin off your face.'

'Aw shucks, Daisy, give him a break. He was only smiling. Honi soit qui mal y pense, that means honey your silk stocking's hanging down. I looked it up.'

Daisy raised her eyes to Heaven.

'Yep, she's a real lady,' Mackenzie added. 'Top of the pile, a virgin forsooth. Snow White, British version.'

'Exactly, a virgin, and don't you forget it,' milady declared. 'I was born in Oxford and died in London. My entire life was devoted to the Royal Family, the Church of England and the Empire – God rest its soul.'

Bob was on his feet now, but swaying.

'He don't look too perky', said Archie. 'He needs cheering up, you scared him.'

A loud buzzing came from the computer, causing the voyager to jump. Lady Daisy leapt to the keyboard and began tapping out Bob's surname.

An image of an operating theatre appeared on the large screen, with a team of medics around the singer as he lay on the table. Treillet pointed to the chief surgeon: 'That's Docteur Koln. He was at my party. I guess he had me flown to his hospital in Marseille after my accident.'

All three watched the scene for a while. Dr. Koln was massaging the patient's chest. Several minutes went by, then Koln stood back satisfied, nodding to his team.

Daisy pushed a button and the picture faded.

'He pulled you through again. You are still alive, young man, and you have no business wasting your time and ours too. Off you go, there's a good lad, I cannot be held responsible if you persist in remaining at the Centre, especially if this blockhead Mackenzie keeps interfering. We wish you a pleasant return journey, Monsieur Treillet. Archibald, come with me, we have work to do.'

Lady Daisy scribbled again on her clipboard and disappeared through the wall, followed by Mackenzie who mimicked her ungainly stride.

Treillet tried to follow but bumped into the wall.

'Malheur,' he cried. 'Those priests were right. God exists, or at any rate something like Him does.'

For eight long years, while he was at boarding school, he'd had a grim time as a boy. The reverend fathers had sought to instruct Robert Treillet in the mysteries of the One True Church by means of verbal repetition, ear twisting and caning on the buttocks. Notwithstanding their diligence, young Robert had remained unresponsive to their good tidings and, what's more, earned disgrace for himself by sowing doubt among his fellow pupils.

The torture of listening to the prior's interminable sermons haunted him well into adulthood. The prior's cassock, too big for his shoulders, gave him the appearance of a black scarecrow, and whenever a nincompoop (his favourite expression) of a schoolboy crossed his path, his protruding eyes looked to Heaven in mute supplication.

Treillet was equally in despair at the efforts of his spiritual directors to improve his outlook via the confessional. One of the fathers, known universally as The Thrasher, constantly ordered him to unburden his soul to him in the sin bin, asking intimate questions concerning Bob's activities between the sheets, and handing out long penances. Since invariably he had already been corporally knouted by the said Thrasher the same day, Treillet strongly suspected that this particular cleric was a descendant of the Marquis de Sade. However that may be, he left the boarding school with a deeply imprinted hatred of all authority, especially if it smelled of incense.

In books from his local library, he was later confirmed in his disgust at the inflicting of all violence and tyranny in the name of a hypothetical divinity. The advancing of the human condition was better served by supporting and engaging in political causes that everybody could identify with. Moreover his revolt, coupled with his liking for provocation, drew him naturally towards an ideology whereby communities lived their lives in their own sweet way in the spirit of good neighbourliness. The repeated attempts by the fathers to knock their version of wisdom into his head led him to promise that, if he ever came face to face with the Creator, he would recommend a complete reshuffle of His executive officers.

Having now apparently reached the threshold of the afterlife, the voyager supposed that the aforesaid confrontation with the Almighty was imminent. So much the better, he deemed, as it gave him the chance to prove that he was able to paddle his own canoe. He needed no saviour, no saints or angels. Least of all did he require an alter ego on his coat tails.

Doubts as to his own self-sufficiency had occurred at times when he learned that this or that former school chum had acquired fame or fortune through the cardinal virtues. Then, he had generally succumbed to the appeals of his Other Self to keep his head down and stick to a quiet life.

More specifically, when he began to achieve a breakthrough in his career as a songster, he became obsessed with the idea that some crank would knife him in the back because of the political content of his songs. In fact, during the week when he was recording his first composition, a punk in the Paris Metro actually lunged at him, and he had taken refuge behind an elderly woman with an umbrella who sent the attacker sprawling with a sharp blow to the cranium. Thereafter he found himself constantly looking round to make sure that nobody, except his shadowy Other Self, was following him with malice aforethought.

In a word, he had lost confidence in himself well before the hostilities commenced with his Other Self. His bouts of anguish tied his innards in knots, so much so that when a bad depression took hold of him he would park his car on some cliff and reflect for hours on the slings and arrows of outrageous fortune, sometimes coming very close to ending them with a decisive jab to the accelerator. The knowledge that it would all be over in a matter of few seconds inevitably sobered him up, and the longer he stayed on the cliff edge the soberer he would become.

So much for the past. Now he was in a fighting mood; and it was a matter of milliseconds after Archie and Daisy had gone before he leapt to the computer keyboard. His intention was to drift through the wall as they had, by means of the computer. But this was easier said than done; either you had to know the code, or you needed a password. The fact is that his bid failed miserably, and after perhaps fifteen minutes he flung himself on the floor of the white-walled room, to bang his fists helplessly on the flagstones.

Once again he was surprised that he didn't feel anything; it was most frustrating. He poked himself all over with a finger and still felt nothing.

At this point he remembered that Daisy had tapped out his surname, and he returned to the keyboard, copying her action.

It worked! A picture of himself flashed onto the wall, depicting him in the hospital, laid out on a bed but still breathing in the intensive care unit.

If he were still alive, what was he doing in this Centre, this other existence? The enigma remained.

He looked closer at the picture and, through the glass partition of the intensive care room, he could see people waiting in the corridor.

'By golly,' he muttered, 'there's Bernard and that's Olga with him.'

Bernard Dubois, younger than Bob by a few years, was his manager and the chief architect of his success in show business. He was plumped forlornly on a stool with his head in his hands. Not only was Bernard well known, he was also a sprightly negotiator accustomed to handling touchy artists as well as tough business colleagues.

Olga Paslov, nearing fifty years of age, was Bob's press agent. Upon the arrival of the Bolsheviks to power, her grandparents, musical advisers of the tsar, were instantly advised to go on whistling Scheherazade on foreign land. French by adoption, Olga remained Russian through to her fingertips. Clad in her biker outfit and her iron fist always ready to strike, she was given the nickname of Domina. She was pacing up and down puffing at a cigarillo. She had been chain smoking, judging by the number of butts in an ashtray next to Bernard, now coughing from the smoke. Olga, who had divorced three times, was doubly interested in the adjacent scene, for she was hoping to marry Dr. Koln the chief surgeon, having met him when he inadvertently sat on her lap in the dark when arriving late for a ballet performance. Koln was a widower and Olga set her sights on him as a possible fourth husband. Bob had encouraged her to the hilt and had become her close friend.

Bob's Other Self disliked Olga, repeatedly warning of trouble ahead, fearing that she might foresake Koln and try to hook Treillet. An incident on the Champs Elysées had cemented their affection. Bob was crossing the avenue with his press agent, day-dreaming and oblivious to the traffic. She pulled him to safety, as they say, from under the wheels of a fire truck. Thereafter she took him in hand like a child, aiding him in moments of despair, sweeping away his doubts, shielding him from the nastier critics. To Olga, who couldn't have children, Bob Treillet was her baby in more senses than one.

Treillet's Other Self need not have worried, for the pop star was not the marrying kind, he was too screwed up psychologically for most women to handle twenty four hours a day. Oh yes, he'd had his adventures, but they were short-lived. Normal red-blooded girls wanted something more between bonks than a tête-à-tête on the European Monetary Union or the North-South Dialogue. Besides, when an intellectually inclined partner gave him as good as he got in the realm of geopolitics, he habitually withdrew from the contest and revealed that he was married with four runny-nosed kids.

Also pacing the hospital corridor was Olga's assistant, Honorine from Guadeloupe. This dark beauty, weighing approximately one tenth of a ton, had lost her parents in a hurricane, and was despatched to relatives running a banana, coconut and sundries discount store in the northern port of Le Havre. Later she married an insurance clerk and regretted it almost at once. To her way of thinking, Bob Treillet was exactly the exciting kind of celebrity she ought to have wed, and when she met him at a press reception, it was love at first sight. Tough luck on her, cupid's arrow missed Treillet's heart, and he repulsed her advances. He continued to do so even after she paid a witch-doctor to put a spell on him.

'No news is good news,' she proferred brightly as she marched up and down the corridor.

Bernard and Olga glared at her.

'Stop clumping around,' Olga growled. 'And don't keep chattering.'

Asking Honorine to keep still was difficult in itself, expecting her to be silent for any length of time was absurd. The need to talk was hormonal in her case, it all had to come out.

Dr. Koln strode out of the intensive care unit, waxen-faced with fatigue. Accompanying him was a Eurasian nurse with breathtaking green eyes. Treillet, perched on high with his eyes on the computer screen, was struck by her beauty – that gaze, the statuesque body, the lilting walk …

'Well how is he?' Honorine squeaked.

'All set for a duo with John Lennon,' the celestially-parked Treillet muttered to himself.

'His condition remains critical,' Koln said levelly.

'Merde alors,' said Bob.

'Multiple trauma, twin fracture of the spine, lesion of the spinal cord,' Koln enumerated gravely.

'Lord! So his brain's affected,' Honorine moaned.

'Third degree coma.'

'Third degree?' she cried. 'Anything else?'

But Koln walked on. Olga dug an elbow into her assistant to keep her quiet. It was like asking a mouse to skip the cheese course. Honorine trotted after Koln.

'He'll be paralyzed, won't he?'

'It's too early to reach a conclusion,' he said.

Treillet from above was beside himself.

'Hey, take it easy. I'm not dead yet, where there's life there's hope.'

Honorine put her hands together in dismay. 'A four hour operation for nothing.'

'What's Koln hemming and hawing about?' growled the ghostly voice of Treillet. 'Let's have some of the old Teutonic discipline, not this shilly-shallying.'

Honorine was still lumbering after the surgeon.

'How long will he be in a coma?'

'Yeah, how long, you snivelling kraut?' echoed Treillet.

'The brain has been seriously affected. We must wait.'

Dr. Koln gave a faint smile as Bernard Dubois gulped audibly.

'In other words he'll never be the same again.'

'We must wait till he comes out of intensive care.'

Olga chewed on a nicotine-stained nail. 'It doesn't look very hopeful. We can't make a press statement yet.'

'In most cases, major brain cell damage is irreversible,' Koln added.

Honorine made a sign of the cross. 'Sweet Jesus, he'd be better off meeting the Almighty.'

'You can say that again,' said the ethereal Treillet. 'I've got a few important questions to ask Him.'

Honorine was a kind-hearted girl. One of her recent ideas, dating from just before the ULM crash, had been to form a Bob Treillet Fan Club. Bernard and Olga had backed the project and so had Treillet himself, but his Other Self had poured cold water on the idea, and the file was still in the pending tray at the office.

Dr. Koln offered a final comment that nobody understood. 'I have done everything I could. Believe me, one of us will win.' He clicked his heels and ambled off.

To avoid the news pack waiting at the main porch of the hospital, Bernard and Honorine made for a side exit. On her way out Honorine pulled a flask from her handbag and took a large swig of rum. She offered the flask to Bernard, who shook his head.

Olga caught Koln up, in her role of bride-to-be. 'What exactly did you mean, one of us will win?'

'I'm fighting death. Each time it's a grim battle, each time I wonder why we have to die at all. We ought to pass away in glory like gods ourselves. I hate losing a patient, watching him die in swinish pain and indignity.'

'I understand, dearest.'

It was the surgeon's wont, if he lost a patient, to spend a while in the morgue going back over the diagnosis and the operation to see where he'd gone wrong. If the patient recovered he would celebrate with a slap-up meal, and Olga knew that.

'How about dinner together?' she said gaily, trying to cheer him up. 'What do you say to champagne sauerkraut? It's your favourite dish, the ham they use at that place is top class.'

'Oh no, thanks all the same. I've seen enough meat for one day,' he said with a bitter laugh. 'Not only did we remove a kidney, we cut his testicles off too. He had a fine pair, the nurses were all eyes. Turned them on, I daresay.'

'That's a horrible thing to say, Franz.'

Treillet, looking down, was livid. 'The bloody sadist. He can't be normal. Turned me into a goddam eunuch and he thinks it's funny.'

He grabbed for his balls, but felt nothing. His Other Self could claim another victory. All right, he'd show them, he'd damn well stay in the Universal Selection Centre, he would not return to his body. No doubt Archie and Daisy would pester him with questions about his past and he would handle that problem when the time came. He need not tell the truth, the whole truth and nothing but the truth. Let them think what they liked.

2

Bernard Dubois had approached Bob one night when he was playing in a piano bar near the harbour at Saint-Tropez. He was drawn not so much to his gravelly voice, comparable with that of an asthmatic crow he opined, as to his compositions. Here, he reckoned, was a politically committed artist, a militant troubadour who might go far having regard to the restless mood of the nation. The bar owner, a Corsican separatist whose main aim was to have the ceremony of the afternoon nap written into the French Constitution pending the setting up of an independent Corsica, had urged him to concentrate on a leftist-cum-anarchist style that would make the headlines and bring them both fame and fortune. Dubois agreed with this angle and spent hours with Bob discussing the brave new world he envisaged, telling him that no-one could do more to rekindle the flickering flame of mankind's hopes. Like Bob Dylan, The Beatles, The Rolling Stones, maybe Treillet and he would start a whole new trend in popular music. It was worth going for.

Bob was indeed the kind of angry young man with whom millions could identify, especially among the new generation. After the implosion of Soviet style communism, and with capitalism facing new difficulties, the dominant system in the West was bound to break up before long, Treillet calculated. The worldwide cash nexus was making the rich richer and the poor poorer, sooner or later the inherent antagonism would lead to street fighting, civil war and the destruction of the artificial civilization now prevailing. Centuries ago Nostradamus the monk had predicted the end of the world around now, and it was a sure thing that a gigantic planetary holocaust lay ahead if nothing were done.

The bigwigs in the pop music trade were not so sure, and Bob was piling up rejection slips that came with his returned compositions. The truth was that they found his revolutionary lyrics pretty old hat, he was half a generation out of step, chasing behind the new yuppie philosophy. His kind of creed was dying out after the May 1968 failed uprising, they claimed.

Both Bernard and Bob had joined the students burning cars and hurling cobblestones in the Paris streets. Bernard was rather ashamed that he later turned bourgeois, and regretted that he hadn't joined the anarchists who went in for 'Action Directe'. He excused himself on the ground that his girlfriend got pregnant and he was forced to marry her. He was a bourgeois only on the surface. Bob himself had personally driven a bus into a line of riot police near the Sorbonne. An act of heroism for his fellow students, an act of terrorism for the law. It earned him two months in the Santé prison.

Delicately and diplomatically, Bernard weaned Treillet from his May 68 nostalgia, explaining that songs looking back to those days had been taken over by the big names in show business. But it wouldn't last much longer. The strategy now was to convert his disturbing stark true-to-life numbers into half-truths interpreted in a way that the Establishment could condone. He claimed that people were looking for exotic escapist music with a good tom-tom rhythm, and a backing line of girls including one or two just coloured enough to suit the media. Then it was a matter of pitching his image just right. Never start out as a loser, that was the secret. Be convincing and don't forget the nice guy angle, he urged.

Bernard wisely omitted to say that the quality need not be outstanding, that a well-marketed CD of a cat on heat would sell these days like condoms from a slot machine on a summer's night. He persuaded Bob there was no harm in making money from an honest living, everyone had to survive in this new crazy mixed up world.

Bob, who had lost several guitar pupils after a breach of promise case involving the daughter of a local councillor, absorbed Bernard's message with surprising ease. Moreover his name was mud in the town because the court case made the local press. Now, he believed, was his chance to hit back in the only way that counted on the Riviera, viz, by getting rich. Overnight his principles went into cold storage, his convoluted ideologies were thrown out with the empty bottles, replaced by the sweet smell of forthcoming success.

Olga Paslov took him in hand as his press agent. Bob's past history and behaviour were carefully rewritten to suit the marketing pitch, his sentiments aligned with those of the anguished youngsters facing unemployment, exclusion and AIDS. When it emerged that he smoked hashish and marijuana, had a liking for young girls half his age and drank like a fish, this was explained away by a recent spiritual retreat in an Indian ashram, where he gained an insight into mystical theory and practice. A mysterious smell of mysticism could only strengthen the credibility of his new personality.

And of course, as with most current pop stars, his standing was enhanced by soundbites on radio and TV in support of humanitarian causes. Africa already counted a lot of ardent defenders involved in numerous causes. However, it was useless to pick out one already adopted by a colleague, and silly to get involved in one too obscure to raise general public interest. Finally, Treillet donated time and money to all kinds of charity events, covering victims of war, disease, natural disaster and wildlife facing extinction.

His management team made sure his every gesture was well publicized until the artist himself called a halt on the grounds that the corruption level was too high. Sickened with the ways of man, he saw himself as a purist turned prostitute, a view encouraged by his Other Self.

In due course Bob was informed by his advisors that he was letting himself go physically. In a word he was putting on weight. He was already a ULM enthusiast, he protested, but Bernard said it was not sensational enough or modern enough to gain publicity and fixed up a sponsor for Bob to race water scooters.

But Treillet was not a happy man. His Other Self kept telling him that he was being promoted more like a detergent or a brand of cornflakes than the rebel troubadour he had set out as. Sacrificing his talent and integrity for the sake of achieving success, Bob couldn't underpin his image of a pure and tough anarchist. Bob, who used to have an opinion about everything, had to settle for having no opinion on anything.

It was at this point that the nationwide scandal occurred. Through a previous husband, an anchorman on a private TV channel, Olga managed to get him a prime time interview after the sports news. Bob handled it badly, admitting to the interviewer at one stage that he was taking the public for a ride. His Other Self whispered that he was heading for disaster in thirty seconds flat, but Bob's taste for provocation prevailed. The anchorman, sensing a scoop, fed him several questions to draw him out, and Treillet finished the chat by turning his back to the camera, lowering his trousers and poking his bum at the viewers, presenting his posterior to posterity, as he simultaneously remarked. Honest citizens from Calais to Bordeaux, from Brest to Menton, were outraged. But the youth of France poured into the music shops, and his latest album was a sell-out.

The upshot was that, for a brief moment, Bob Treillet was top of the pops. Even so, he was thenceforth as popular as a po in a hotel foyer, as far as the media was concerned. His star shone briefly like a comet, and disappeared from the show business firmament just as fast.

In the white-walled room at the Universal Selection Centre, the lost voyager eyed the computer suspiciously. The hospital scene was of little interest at the moment, as nothing seemed to be going on. Even so, he left the picture on.

The minutes went by, or at least he imagined they did, even if he assumed that time did not exist on the edge of eternity. He'd once had a long argument with an astronomy fanatic who claimed there was no time in eternity, and Bob told him to prove it, and the other man told Bob to prove the contrary; the outcome was inconclusive, with each telling the other that the onus of proof lay with the proposer. In the end, Bob stalked off saying he didn't have time to waste.

Suddenly, the screen went off. Archie and Daisy wafted in, coming to a halt in front of Treillet.

'Monsieur Treillet!' bawled Daisy. 'You ought to be back on Earth. Why are you hanging about like this? The U.S.C. is not a hotel, you realize.'

Bob's eyes narrowed: 'I'm not budging from here until I know why I am here in the first place. If there's been a mistake I demand compensation and a full inquiry. I hereby demand to see my lawyer!'

'Pshaw!' Daisy exclaimed.

'You see the state I'm in, castrated, my manhood cut off in youth.'

He looked down, pulled up his tunic and showed them.

'Look, no marbles!'

The other two shrugged as he added: 'I'm finished, a physical wreck, a mental ruin, a soul without a purpose. Sorry, I simply can't go on, I just want to disappear for ever, to become a bit of cosmic dust going down a black hole.'

'Monsieur Treillet,' Daisy persisted in a rather kinder tone. 'We can sympathize with your predicament but are sadly in no position to help you. As far as the Centre is concerned, you have neither body nor soul. To put it plainly, we don't know you. So be a good boy, get back into your body and obtain the right documents.'

'Documents?'

'Yes. Bumpf,' Archie said, 'I think they call it that in the British army. Or is it something more colourful. Anyhow, you must go through the proper channels. It's like this, chum, you are here because someone made a snap decision in a moment of emotional strain for you. Don't ask me who he was. If you return to Earth you can cancel it.'

Treillet drummed his fists on his skull. 'This is crazy. We are all going stark raving mad. What's the point of going back to the hospital if I'm already up here? Can't you phone them and get the documents faxed, or something? Down there they will simply shunt me around, you don't know the French civil service. I shall be back here, back to square one as it were.'

'Nothing personal,' said Archie. 'Zior makes the decisions here.'

'And who the blazes is Zior when he's home?'

'Our spiritual leader,' Daisy replied with unctuous respect.

Zior was in fact an invisible entity and was never seen. In a jocular moment, Archie had suggested to Daisy that he might be a hermaphrodite. Certainly there was no guessing Zior's sex as he/she/it had an electronic voice, but they called him 'he' for convenience.

To Daisy's chagrin, Archie sometimes played tricks on her, imitating Zior's voice. He once 'ordered' Daisy to do a belly dance; Archie's motive was to help her surmount her puritan mental blocks. She obeyed the command as best she could, until Archie gave himself away by slipping into his natural Brooklyn accent and telling her: 'We'll let you know; sugar-puss, don't call us we'll call you.'

Daisy at once lodged a complaint with Zior, who told her the case was 'not in my precinct'. It was for them to sort out their metaphysical issues, they could try Kant or Sartre on existential riddles. Zior also said that Archie and Daisy must continue their efforts to achieve a higher spiritual status; souls reaching the Centre must throw off their earthly short-comings before approaching the Divine Light, death was no passport to beatitude. Above all, they had to learn how to filter It, to comprehend It, in order to diffuse It afterwards. At their poor level of evolution, the Divine Light remained an energy impossible to describe as well as quite incomprehensible.

Fervently Church of England, Daisy identified the Divine Light with the God of the Christians, just as a Muslim would compare Him to Allah or an Asian to Buddha. Whether the term Divine Light or Supreme Power was used, Daisy co-opted It to Anglican doctrine and continued resolutely to find the adequate evidence in scripture.

Zior had to remind her that religions stemmed from the habit of human beings to create God in their image, with the result that they went on murdering one another in God's name. The truth of the matter, concluded Zior, was that God was universal and mankind would be much better off without killing one another in His name.

Having divulged all this, Zior left them to stew in their own semantic juice. For Daisy, who liked to classify everything meticulously, referring to A Divine Light instead of A God Almighty was too much for her. With his usual sense of derision, Archie suggested they call It the Supreme Power. Daisy, shocked but having no better suggestion, had to agree.

Now she turned to Treillet. 'So you refuse to leave, as I understand it young man, until you know as much as we do. Unfortunately, voyagers like yourself are not equipped to perceive the invisible. That, by the way, is why Zior approved Archibald's scheme for plastic bodies so that you would be on familiar ground, as it were. Of course, this artificial body doesn't eat, defecate and so on.'

'Tough luck old chap,' Archie cackled. 'No more oysters, caviar, Chateauneuf du Pape – and no more hangovers.'

'Oh, do be quiet,' Daisy snapped. 'How can you be so so stupid?'

'Well, it ain't easy milady ...'

'Listen both of you,' Treillet said wearily. 'Before you two arrived at this Centre, you were human beings, I take it.'

They nodded with a faint smile.

'And now you are extraterrestrials of a sort. How long ago did you die?'

'Can't really say,' Archie replied. 'There is no time span here.'

Bob soldiered on: 'And this argument of yours about Divine Light and Supreme Power. You're talking about God, right?'

'Words, words,' Archie hooted, flapping a hand. 'The mystery of all mysteries. To be or not to be, as Shakespeare wrote. Ever since Zior posted us here we've been waiting to be kicked upstairs. Then we shall see the Big Boss, the Godfather as you might say.'

'What nonsense,' Daisy snorted. 'Typically American of you to relate solemn facts with the delicacy of a mobster.'

Treillet ploughed on: 'It seems to me that you are in some kind of purgatory, parked on the side of the road. Correct me if I'm wrong.'

Daisy cleared her throat, gave a sniff and fiddled with her skirt: 'It's more of a research centre here to do with the human condition. You must realize that all those questions that worry people when they are alive have no importance at the U.S.C. You'll get nowhere by interrogating us in this aggressive way. You can keep on until doomsday but we are pledged to secrecy. The information you seek is confidential, not for prying eyes. Besides, you know as much as we do.'

'She's right, you know,' said Archie.

'She sounds like Alice in Wonderland. All these evasive replies make me sick,' their guest mumbled hopelessly.

Archie tried to help. 'The Supreme Power is not interested in money and success, even less in power. He has his own values, and our little problems just don't concern him.'

'Monsieur Treillet,' Daisy added. 'We are being very considerate with you, but there is a limit to our patience. I repeat, we cannot accommodate you here in your present state. It goes without saying that, when you are officially deceased, your case will be reconsidered. You will probably then be greeted by your dear ones who preceded you, when you emerge from the tunnel with the right documents. At least that's the official procedure, although in your case anything might happen. Your whole attitude is wrong as far as I can see, and you must conform. I myself was greeted personally by Zior,' she said with pride. 'Now go back to Earth at once, or Zior will surely punish you. I hope that's plain enough.'

She turned, ready to disappear through the wall: 'My poor boy, there's none so dim as will not understand.'

Daisy pranced off, with Archie in tow imitating her gait.

The disheartened voyager in transit again picked out his name on the computer keyboard and the hospital intensive care unit once more appeared on the screen. Something was happening. The Eurasian nurse in Dr. Koln's team was studying the patient's dossier, waggling her head this way and that in the Gallic way, evidently worried.

Bob moved closer to the picture and his eyes widened. She had emerald green eyes, an ivory complexion, jet black hair and a slim body that no normal European male could ignore. Alas he was no longer normal without his goolies. Bob vowed that, when all this was over, he would write a song for her and call it Emerald.

She looked up from the dossier and managed a weak smile so enchanting that Treillet audibly caught his breath.

Then he realized that her smile was for a tall handsome junior doctor on the other side of the bed, and a stab of jealousy surged through him. He'd have liked to know her name. He assumed that she had reached France in the wake of the Indochina wars. This increased his desire, he could never resist a pretty girl in need of comfort.

Treillet had paid the price of spontaneous love many times. Years before at the Beaux Arts academy in Paris he had fallen for an Italian archaeology student. While the girl scrabbled around in the capital's catacombs, Bob had taken lessons in Indian music, which was coming into vogue at the time under the influence of the Khatmandu factor. The idyll went on for several weeks and Treillet thought fit to ask her hand in marriage. The signorina had other ideas, she was unwilling to link up with a combatant in the anarchist business. The budding musician had persisted in his wooing for a few more weeks behaving like the perfect Romeo, but his Juliet was not bitten by the anarchist bug. When she finally dismissed him with a flea in his ear, he believed in all logic that his only course was to repeat the Romeo knife trick and quit his mortal frame. But youth tends to be resilient and he merely resolved to separate sex from romance thereafter, for better or worse. It was then that the notion first struck him of avoiding sentimental ditties and embarking on 'committed music'.

Shortly afterwards he knocked up a Dutch girl. Her dad decided that he was too young to be a grandad and an abortion was arranged.

Following this contretemps, a friend of Bob's, who was fed up practising as a midwife and wanted to become a coroner, advised him to tie a knot in it, or in more technical terms to have a vasectomy. His Other Self, of a paternal nature, warned that he was storing up trouble for the future, but Bob's present troubles carried more weight and the operation took place.

As a means of letting off steam, he took up golf, showing a preference for lady partners. Weather permitting he played the 19th hole as often as not, holing in one.

When the dark dank days of winter arrived, Bob imposed on himself long periods of abstinence in order to prove his willpower to his Other Self. He disliked the proliferation of TV commercials for stockings and underwear, salacious talk shows, more or less phony statistics on the sexual performance of men. All this junk information made people believe that most males were interested only in tits and arses. Strangely enough, he was totally bewildered on sighting the delectable Eurasian on the screen. Having made a hash of his love life so far, castrated and with more than a foot in the grave, it was astonishing that he had any libido left at all, he reflected. If the chemistry of concupiscence went on dogging the near-dead, human nature had little chance of resisting it, apparently.

When spring came around again, the golf course ladies took over once more for another round of practice founded not so much on theory as on pent-up celibacy.

In the realm of politics Bob had trouble with his parents, who eventually told him to give up his revolutionary nonsense, or never to darken their door again. When he refused, they showed him the doorstep. He took to the road and roamed all over France with a guitar and knapsack, thus to make his fortune. Avoiding towns, all summer long he would strum and sing his way through villages, bemusing tractor drivers and milkmaids with lugubrious ballads of a Che Guevara flavour. When the autumn leaves fell, he found odd jobs mucking out cowsheds and mending fences in exchange for a bite to eat, a bottle of cheap red wine and a bed of straw among the agricultural implements.

As sheep may stray, so did young Treillet. He enjoyed the life, it was true freedom, life as it should be lived. True happiness lay in rejecting the affluent society and adopting the nomadic existence, and he was proving it. The philosophy shuddered to a halt when his parents died in an aircrash and he inherited not only their cottage, but also their hotel and café business, which he sold off. Overnight he became a bourgeois property owner and a capitalist investor, whether he liked it or not.

His parents never had much use for him. He was packed off as a boy to a remote holiday camp in the Alps so that he wouldn't clutter up the hotel and café during the tourist season. His old man tried to interest him in the business, deploring his lazing around singing bolshie ballads, but when he laid aside his guitar it was only to play with their alsatian dog stationed permanently outside the building to scare off beggars. In the face of their indifference to his musical talents, he wondered why they had bothered to bring him into the world at all, since they never displayed the slightest affection towards him.

Bob was shaken out of his reveries by a voice that was becoming only too familiar to him. Daisy was back with Archie whistling his favourite song New York, New York.

'Are you still here?' she bellowed. 'You're out of your mind, I must be dreaming.'

She advanced on him and he cowered into a corner. Mackenzie now hummed a few bars of When I Grow Too Old to Dream.

'It's you who are out of your mind,' Treillet squeaked. 'You must be crackers to imagine I'd go back down there in my mutilated circumstances. I wouldn't have the cheek to impose myself on others without the use of my limbs, with my undercarriage shot away.'

'Rubbish, you are too wrapped up in yourself to have genuine friends.'

Bob darted forward and was eyeball to eyeball with her.

'Thanks for nothing. Every human being has a right to run his own life as he thinks fit. Take another look at the Declaration of Human Rights!'

'You must be joking,' Archie whooped.

Daisy bared her teeth and growled: 'While you are in the U.S.C., my boy, the only right you have is to do what you are told. You play ball with us and we'll play ball with you.'

'Nom d'un chien, don't mention balls to me ever again.'

'Regulation 1-A states that voyagers in transit who overstay their time risk clinical death,' she persisted.

'Really, and what do the other regulations say?'

'There aren't any others. So far you have been a privileged observer of your own coma, and you'll end up seeing that coma change to clinical death if you stay. Actual death will inevitably follow. Don't ask us how long it will take, it's not our problem!'

'You can't blackmail me.'

'You tried to blackmail us,' Archie pointed out.

'If you insist on remaining at the Centre, I must remind you that clinical death is irreversible,' Daisy said solemnly with an evil glint in her eye. 'You will be in a vegetative phase at the hospital and meanwhile you will be stuck here powerless to influence the course of events. So much for your supposed right to live your own life. Human Rights, indeed!'

'You will be impotent twice over,' Archie volunteered.

'Every minute that goes by,' Daisy warned, 'means that you have less chance of pulling through.'

'Oh yeah, and stop wagging your finger at me.'

'There is a simple reason for that. Your body needs mental effort by yourself to emerge from a coma. Your survival is in the balance, you are between two stools, your life is on the razor's edge, so don't sit on the fence. There is a point of no return, Treillet, don't you forget it.'

'It sounds highly uncomfortable, the way you put it. A razor's edge, sitting on a fence between two stools.'

Behind her back, Mackenzie was mimicking her every gesture.

'Stop prancing around, Archibald.'

'Me?' Archie retorted innocently. 'I was only thinking you must have scared the nuts off those footmen at the palace.'

'I'd cut them off you if you had any.'

Treillet gave a cough: 'Excuse me for interrupting this exalted conversation, but I wonder if I might try my luck with this computer of yours. Where new technology is concerned I'm still at the hammer and nail stage, but it's never too late to learn.'

'And you may not have much time left,' she quipped, reeling off a cascade of hideous glee. 'Let's get this straight, I am prepared at a pinch to suffer the jibes of Archibald Mackenzie, who was a professional clown, but I won't let you mock one of the most senior officials of the royal household. Besides, you have already made use of the computer without my permission. If you want to have another look at your miserable state down there, go ahead, twist the knife in the wound.'

She was off again, shrieking with inane laughter.

Bob renewed his enquiries: 'As a matter of interest, can one look in on other people, strangers?'

'Certainly not. This equipment is for one purpose, checking on voyagers during their comas on Earth. And now I must leave you.'

'Er, where are you going now?' Bob asked, suddenly feeling fearful at being left alone.

'We are going to report to Zior about your pig-headed attitude. The spiritual director will be furious when he hears that you are here. Archie, come with me, but kindly spare us your silly imitations, you're behaving like a warthog on heat these days. Very odd that you still have such a raging sex drive considering your condition.'

'Huh, huh,' said Archie. 'Better than a menopause that's gone sour.'

They disappeared through the wall, and the voyager from Earth tried to follow them as before, only to bump up hard against the wall. As before he felt no pain and shook his head in disbelief. He put his tongue out at the place where they'd left, wiggling his fingers with his thumbs against his temples, finally making a two-finger sign.

This little revolt boosted his morale to some extent, and he wandered over to the computer, to stand before the keyboard with his arms crossed like some owl watching a spaceship just landed from Mars. He found it curious that the equipment should perform only one function. Of course, the old bitch might just have said that to put him off.

With nothing to lose, he tapped out the name of Bernard Dubois, his manager.

Immediately a message came on the screen: Restricted area. No path. Ends.

Too bad it didn't work. It would have been nice to know if his manager was thinking of him down there. Who else could he try? Other? His Other Self? That would be interesting.

He tapped out: Other. The screen read: Other command incomplete. Identify.

Brightening at this, he told the machine: 'Other Self, Homo sapiens species. Male. Born April 1, 1949. He got the result: Other Self. See birth list at that date in Paris.

Oh boy, now we were getting somewhere. He tapped again and a list began rolling down the screen:

Brun Jean, artistic painter

Dufour Raoul, chartered accountant

Grato Paul, plumber

Latour François, truck driver, (deceased)

Treillet Robert, musician (in transit)

Warden John, politician

The screen instructed him: Compare Other Self with above names.

He played a while on the keyboard and got pictures of:

1) A painter in his studio, mixing colours on a palette.
2) An accountant in his office having a nervous breakdown while checking out the State budget.
3) A plumber with an arm thrust down a toilet bowl.
4) A coffin, presumably with the truck driver inside.
5) Himself on the hospital bed.

6) An American senator in a limousine.

This last name rang a bell in his memory. A picture appeared showing a traffic sign indicating Washington's Dulles Airport and advertisement billboards along the road carrying a portrait of a grinning John Warden with the message: 'Vote Warden for a new kind of America'.

He had seen media reports of the young charismatic senator, bidding for the U.S. presidency. Warden was born in France during his father's years as U.S. ambassador in Paris. Analysts across the Atlantic gave him only an outside chance against the others in the race. Bob had noticed him because he was backed by numerous artists, ecologists, anti-nuke scientists and the like. Warden was an advocate of government by introspective democracy, a programme understood by practically no-one, but basically stemming from the economic theory that every person makes decisions in his or her own interests. His main slogan was 'Make happiness not money', and it had stuck in Bob's mind. He recalled too the candidate's pledge to make Wall Street an avenue paved with Big Mac burgers.

This last was a great idea, to Bob's way of thinking. Hadn't someone wrapped the Berlin Reichstag in plastic sheeting? Wasn't Wall Street at the root of the world's ills? The candidate's outspoken speeches had sent shudders through the leadership of the Group of Seven – the world's seven richest countries, and the Dow Jones Industrial Average see-sawed wildly as Senator Warden's fortunes in the opinion polls ebbed and flowed.

Oh what a lovely world it would be if the planet's most powerful nation were to be headed by a man like Warden, whose ideas so closely matched his own.

The voyager's musings were cut short when the screen went blank, to be replaced by the four letters Z I O R. The image gradually came into better focus and he saw Archie and Daisy sitting on a bench in a narrow room like those in a police station entrance. The pair sat stiffly and neither of them was speaking. The name Zior kept flashing like an electric sign.

So they had got as far as Zior's outer office. Bob gulped, his future was about to be decided, he supposed.

On arrival at the Universal Selection Centre, her ladyship had complained to the spiritual director that her death had been premature. It had caused her a nervous breakdown, and she refused to believe that she was no longer alive. Zior had told her that this was a common reaction among people who died without warning, who had dropped dead at the drop of a hat as he put it.

Archie too had ended life's journey in the twinkling of an eye, but he made less fuss over the event. While rejecting organized religion, Mackenzie was not averse to exploring the after-life; in fact he was even attracted to the idea of reincarnation and had fun choosing what he'd like to be in the future existence – a cat perhaps, because of its nine lives, a sacred cow free to wander and chew at what it liked, a bird of paradise, even a boy going like a bunny with all the girl rabbits.

But evidently the authorities had other plans for him and Daisy.

Zior had assigned them a specific mission, which was to persuade voyagers caught between life and death to return to Earth. They were really quite proud to be posthumous sentries and they struck up quite a friendship with their spiritual director.

When Zior had, for example, been agreeable to Archie's idea for artificial bodies to keep the voyagers company, he also agreed that Archie could have his body back in due course.

Mackenzie had been cremated and a friend had scattered his ashes over New York from the top of the Empire State Building in a gale. That way, if reincarnated, he would feel quite at home. Nostalgia makes wishful thinkers of us all. Archie believed in the American Dream, which was fast developing from a melting pot to become a giant pressure cooker. Yes indeed, the good old U.S.A. simply bubbled with exciting activity and Mackenzie meant to be part of it – the black Islamics, the gay community of California, the next generation of Microsoft's Windows – the whole darned human saga rolled into one.

Archie's life in New York was full of surprises, nice and lousy. The nicest had been a contract for a Broadway show that had all the right ingredients for a huge success. The lousy moments included an encounter with druggies short of a snort who flashed knives and relieved him of his ready cash. He adored strolling around the city's avenues – Park, Madison, Columbus, Fifth, as if he owned them all. How refreshing too when you found a spot in Central Park free of exhaust fumes, and if you didn't it was just too bad, the pollution smelled better there with a flavour of its own. New York was the best place to be alive in. Broadway itself thrilled him, it was his very own drug, causing his heartbeat to race with each raising of the curtain.

He had created a dance academy with only a score or so of carefully picked pupils each time, ten boys and ten girls. He liked the girls to be pretty and he hand-picked those if they let him. He was a good teacher and the youngsters graduating from the academy did him credit. The public loved nothing better than to see a ballet based on Ravel's Bolero danced in the nude. Archie would tell the boys and girls they need have nothing to hide; nakedness was the natural condition of human beings, otherwise babies would enter this world in fur coats or leather jeans, but the Almighty had decreed things otherwise and they should throw off their inhibitions with their clothes.

One day a former pupil, who became a star sought after by leading producers, suggested Mackenzie do the choreography for Manhattan Follies, which was to be a look back to the best songs and dances of the past, ending with the celebrated New York, New York. Knowing him, the producer put a clause in his contract stating that, if Mackenzie gave in to his notoriously powerful libido and molested any of the girls, he would be replaced by a younger man, preferably a homosexual.

Daisy, now Archie's colleague, was a completely different case. Her ladyship, who was no oil painting and admitted it, had no wish to rejoin her body, currently mouldering in the grave. The prospect of dragging her angular and creaking corpus derelictum around with her for all time filled her with dismay. On arrival at the Centre she felt that she had been there for centuries already.

She was quickly bored with her own company and soon asked Zior for a companion. 'This is no Garden of Eden,' Zior pointed out, but he gave in and told her to pick a partner. Using computer-aided dating, she came up with Mackenzie, with disastrous consequences from the word go. Theoretically they were complementary, that is to say they had nothing in common. Their meeting was an affair of hatred at first sight, an electric encounter with sparks flying from the outset. Later she admitted that they would have made a better job of their existence together by communicating via the electronic information highway rather than by word of mouth. As every schoolchild knew, the United States and the United Kingdom were nations divided by a common tongue.

Reminding them of the latter, Zior told them to keep the talk to a minimum. Archie found this to his liking, wanting only a quiet life now that he was dead, with plenty of opportunity to re-live in his mind his eventful New York existence. Daisy was more frustrated than ever, she felt a curse on her, and Archie said that was because she was a woman. It was the subject of their first stand up argument. Archie like amiabilities about the weather, the time of day, dogs fouling the sidewalk and the noise level of the neighbour's TV set, which he saw as part of the cosmic plan. Daisy's concerns were more controversial and ranged from the Queen Mother's hat for the Ascot races to the seating arrangements for a 523-guest banquet, which she regarded as infinitely more important within the context of geopolitical trends. It was she who took command of the Centre ipso facto. And, since Archie challenged her every pronouncement, their partnership was Hell on Earth only ten times worse.

Another bone of contention was Mackenzie's vulgarity and his obsession with s-e-x, a word that her ladyship employed only with the greatest difficulty. His ribald conversation and lack of taste confirmed her belief that there were three categories of American; the underclass without anything, the middle class which she considered boring and without imagination and the rich whose obsession with money left them without saving graces. That explained, she told him, how they came to elect presidents who grew peanuts, acted in B movies, and played the saxophone. To which Mackenzie retorted that this was an improvement on the British leadership which had been clobbering the Irish bog dwellers for eight centuries, no less.

Not to be outdone, Daisy argued that the worsening of the world situation since Britain won World War Two stemmed from the export of Yankee cola drinks, popcorn and the proliferation of Burger Kings to what was once 'the most civilized society ever established' under British rule. As that great statesman Burke had rightly said, 'her ancestors had turned a savage wilderness into a glorious empire,' no wonder the sun never ceased to shine on it. The Americans had turned it into a pigsty.

Mackenzie protested and told her that she might have been stuck with a less convivial companion than a Broadway choreographer, for example one of her bagpipe-squalling nancy boys in a kilt. At least he would have been a European, Daisy sniffed, complaining that 'the trouble with you people is that you have no history, which is why you are massacring the English language. You are all immigrants, except the Red Indians, and they only grunt.'

On another occasion she vaunted European culture with a recitation of La Fontaine's The Grasshopper and the Ant in impeccable French. 'You sure make a good grasshopper with that accent of yours,' Archie jested, crooning a verse of Parlez-moi d'Amour into the bargain.

When she was first confronted with Mackenzie dressed in one of his prototype plastic suits, she doubled up laughing as he stuck out his chest and rolled his shoulders, prancing around like some two-year-old. He thought she looked pretty funny too in her frumpy old clothes, and in less than no time they were both chortling away fit to burst. Later, Zior told them each to choose two sets of clothing. Archie now had his suit of tails and his bowler hat, plus another more sober outfit. Daisy kept to her palace gear, hiding away her other set of garments.

Just for the heck of it, Mackenzie sometimes presented himself to her in the nude, whereat she raised her eyes to Heaven and would declaim the collect for the day from the Book of Common Prayer dating from Tudor times. Archie, who did not want to be contaminated by her foolish religious fervour, hastily put on his clothes.

Archie and Daisy decided that they had nothing in common and could scarcely stand each other's presence.

The pair resented Zior's decision to make them work in the same service. They were fundamentally opposed in character, hardly capable of tolerating each other, to say the least. Zior might as well have asked a snake to share its bed with a mongoose. Daisy saw Archie as a snake, while Archie pledged he would deal with her mongoose fashion. Yet he contented himself with recalling that the mongoose, despite its superb agility, was not immunized against snake poison and that a single bite was enough to knock it out.

Her ladyship daily implored the Supreme Power to shorten her suffering, in His infinite mercy. Her colleague, not of the praying kind, resorted to the façade of derision that had caused him so much trouble on Earth.

The leopard can't change its spots, he reflected, aside from which it was too late for him to effect a conversion at this late date. In any case the heavenly powers were inclined toward sick jokes, if the farcical goings-on that they permitted on Earth were indication. Zior had pointed out that humans had the inestimable advantage of having a form of intelligence, and had chosen not to intervene in human affairs, except on rare occasions. Zior had also observed that, among the multifarious forms of life in the immensity of the Universe, humans were in top place when it came to stupidity. Nobody is born perfect, Archie had replied.

Daisy found Archie's blasphemous attitude absurd. He might well laugh at her spinsterish ways but she was deeply shocked that he should dare to mock the divine powers. Zior did not seem over worried at Archie's shafts of so-called wit, but she was certain that Mackenzie would bring down the deity's wrath upon them. Her warnings merely produced rude signs from her colleague, whereat she would blanch at the spectre of Satan's horns and cloven feet, trying to counter the Evil One with prayer and supplication, even venturing a few non-Anglican signs of the cross on occasions.

Throughout her life on Earth, Daisy had strictly respected tradition and given unswerving obedience to her superiors. She had no intention of changing her behaviour now that she was so close to the Supreme Power. Confident in her exemplary conduct so far, she considered the company of her depraved American companion was an unwarranted and intolerable trial. She ceaselessly delved her conscience to discover what the Good Lord had against her.

Archie kept telling her that it was she who understood nothing, being narrow-minded beyond belief. It was his opinion that the Supreme Power and his friends had a horror of such persons, who practised charity and good works solely in order to win a place in Paradise.

Mackenzie had led a rollicking existence, sneering at accepted morality. He was an old goat on the rampage and was proud of it. While on Earth he had never seriously concerned himself with the question of life after death, it was not something he cared to investigate. He had no idea who would ask him to account for his dissolute behaviour, and kept an open mind on spiritual matters. He certainly wasn't prepared to accept reproaches from a toffee-nosed bigot who poked around in a theological lucky dip.

To return to the present, the unhappy pair sitting in silence on the bench awaiting Zior's summons were the picture of misery.

But eventually Mackenzie dared to speak: 'Y'know, Daisy old girl, maybe this Treillet guy has been planted on us for some reason. Maybe he's some kind of FBI agent or from the

CIA, maybe we're gonna be stuck with him.'

'I sincerely hope not. A Frenchman, for pity's sake. They're such awkward people, always arguing; show a Frenchman a rusty nail and he'll gabble on about it for hours. Come to think of it, he does have a garlic and vin rouge smell about him, or am I imagining things? They have a disgusting habit of flicking cherry stones into women's bosoms, even their royals used to do it, I once read in a history book.'

'Never mind, cherie,' her colleague said. 'It's probably the first time that he's seen a bosom made out of steel mesh. I can't imagine his reaction if you showed him your chastity belt.'

Daisy jabbed an elbow sharply into Archie's ribs.

'Take it easy, that's my heart you're playing with,' he coughed. 'Here's a riddle for you. What's the difference between death and love? Well, death is a hole in the heart and love is a hole in your fanny! Go on laugh, you sourpuss, it'll do you good.'

As Daisy's eyes closed tight in embarrassment, Archie went on: 'What if Zior allows the pop singer to stay on?'

'It's possible. He's a special case, that's obvious.'

'So you've taken a fancy for him after all. Zior won't bend the rules.'

'All I ask is that the case be handled as humanely as possible. Our duty is to give every assistance to these voyagers halfway between life and death.'

Archie gave her a mischievous glance: 'You're sure you don't have a personal interest and want to get your hooks on him?'

'Stop insinuating, you naughty man. I don't know what you are talking about.'

'I'm willing to bet you're more concerned about your own feelings than with his.'

'Nonsense!'

'You just want to be rid of me. You want Zior to have Treillet replace me, or else for me to look after him and leave you to your prayers.'

'That's an idea,' she returned, tossing her head.

‘By the way, Daisy, where’s your book of requests to Zior? Got it with you?’

‘I shall record everything when this is over, including your stupid remarks. Don’t worry, my memory is more alive than ever.’

Mackenzie regularly dropped hints to Daisy in an attempt to sweeten up her arid soul. But she wouldn’t budge, standing firm and invincible as the Tower of London. She simply refused to countenance that she might be wrong in her views, that there were at least two sides to every question.

Daisy, for her part, sought in vain to raise the standard of their conversation. Her colleague, however, was as interested in quality as a randy goat on a spring morning half way up the Matterhorn.

‘It would suit you I’m sure if Treillet hung around the Centre for a bit longer. I’ll bet my Mickey Mouse underpants to your Queen Victoria bloomers.’

Archie switched to his electronic imitation of Zior: ‘This is Zior, I can see you now, Lady Daisy. I’d be obliged if you would provide me with a full report. And it’d better be accurate.’

In a decidedly unladylike gesture, Daisy put her tongue out at Mackenzie.

Treillet meanwhile was taking another peak at himself, as portrayed on the computer screen. Through narrowed eyes he scanned the space around his inert earthly body, in case his Other Self was lurking there, wishing his death perhaps.

The only person there was the Eurasian nurse with the green eyes. She was changing the IV bag suspended over his head. He was really quite crazy about her, and he began trying out a few notes in his mind for the song he planned to write for her.

He noticed on closer inspection that she was wearing an identity badge on her uniform. He could just make out the name Emerald.

‘Well, there’s a thing,’ he breathed in awe. ‘Her name really is Emerald. I’ve got an Other Self, but I never knew I had second sight.’

Tenderly the nurse pulled the cover over his upper torso. Treillet felt his eyes smarting. She was the loving mother, the kind sister he never had. And the kind of girl friend he ought to have.

3

Mackenzie and Daisy shared an office at the Universal Selection Centre. Down the middle was a thick white line marking the frontier between them. Archie called it the demilitarized zone.

The pair were in a studious mood. Archie had pushed aside his crossword puzzle and was slumped in his chair with his feet up on the desk, examining Treillet's file. Daisy meanwhile read the account of Mary Magdalene's repentance in the New Testament.

The list that Daisy submitted for approval to Zior for the decoration of her part of her office had a French Second Empire desk and a lifesize crucifix on the wall, two big candles, a prayer stool and a straw mattress. A selection of religious paintings completed the decor. As opposed to her space that looked like a chapel of rest, Mackenzie's territory was more in the nature of a student's bedsit, with a white plywood board on a couple of trestles for a desk. His chair was a replica of a movie director's, with his name on the back. His bed consisted of a sleeping bag on a gymnast's exercise pad. He had spotlights beaming harshly down on the area, which had two Greek urns, the statue of a Zulu in a state of erection, and posters of vaudeville shows featuring young ladies in feathers with their bottoms out to one side. There was also a large photo of the late Humphrey Bogart signed by Humph himself.

Some time previously Daisy had complained to Zior about the Zulu, saying it was disgusting. Archie complained about the crucifix, saying it was an object of papist idolatry. He'd get rid of the randy Zulu, if she dumped the crucifix.

'Over my dead body,' Daisy bellowed.

Zior declined to intervene and the two items remained, eyeing each other from opposite walls.

When they weren't attending to newly-arrived voyagers, they were supposed to meditate, but in practice they spent most of their time finding fault with each other.

Daisy longed to be back in Buckingham Palace carrying out her duties instead of being cooped up here with her debauched maniac of a colleague. Having worked her way up from assistant keeper of the royal powder room to the position of mistress of the royal household, she had more than 100 staff under her control at the time of her demise. By single mindedness and willpower she had risen to the pinnacle of her profession and was proud to have done it virtually without help from anyone. She knew that the monarchy knew they could rely on her.

Her personnel she ruled with an iron hand. Archie would often tease Daisy for, as he imagined, torturing her staff on the rack, thrashing them with a cat o' nine tails for impertinence, and throwing them into the dungeons. Repeatedly he threatened to hang, draw and quarter milady, in the good old fashioned way. And when she could take no more of this sarcasm she would open the wardrobe which they shared, and weigh into his trousers with a coathanger, aiming at the crotch and hissing: 'Take that you filthy beast, and that and that and that!' Archie would pretend to howl with pain and cry out: 'Yes, yes, do it again, ten times more and I'll add a coupla hundred bucks!'

Her severity towards the eight male voyagers who had turned up at the Centre since her own arrival had terrified them, and they had been only too glad to hasten back to their earthly bodies. She had sent away four Americans, two Japanese, an Irishman and a Pakistani from somewhere North of Watford. And now there was this dreadful Frenchman. Zior had tricked her, telling her she should keep up her French language skills, and then Treillet had burst in on them shortly afterwards. Her great fear now was that the Centre would be overrun with horny young peacocks all talking like Maurice Chevalier and making her life a misery. Why oh why did they always have to be men? One could have such pleasant chats with women, they were such delightful company as compared with the males of the species who were for ever fighting and risking their lives and turning the world upside down. No wonder they had so many near-death experiences.

Archie himself was a real pain in the neck, constantly provoking her, probing her for shortcomings during her life on Earth. While Daisy was occasionally prepared to admit to a venial sin here and there, she had wisely staved off anything in the nature of in-depth psychoanalysis. Any wrong doing, supposed or otherwise, was a matter between her and her Maker, she contended.

Mackenzie claimed that he himself had nothing to hide, and gloried in his scandalous past, pouring tales of his amorous conquests into her chaste ears. He had no objection to the British as such and felt sure that Daisy was far from a typical example. Back in the States she would certainly have been a leading light in the women's rights brigade. Come to think of it, her ridiculous aversion to men could perhaps hide something more sinister, maybe she was a lesbian and didn't know it!

Being a sentimental fellow of a festive turn in mind, Mackenzie called for a week's truce each Christmas. Much good did it do, for Daisy continued treating him like a pile of shit and the yuletide passed by as grimly as the rest of the year. This being so, one New Year's Night in a desperate bid to create a modicum of goodwill he crossed the white line, grabbed Daisy as she was reading about the ox and the ass, and started whirling her around in a frenetic rock and roll. Daisy boxed his ears and without more ado he laid her across his knees, pulled up her skirt and administered her a right royal spanking.

She was devastated and said he was a beast, a wicked and slimy pervert and she ordered him to get back to his kennel.

She had never been so humiliated in her whole life. From that point on, she not only hated him but she meant to despise him with a passion.

With his foot on the top of his desk, Mackenzie mimicked her in a high falsetto: 'Oh, venerable Zior, be merciful to dear Bobby, we beseech thee; in thy great wisdom let him stay, let me rest a soothing hand upon his troubled brow. Male and female created He them. . .'

He changed to his normal voice: 'You've got the hots on him, admit it!'

'You're stark raving mad.'

'Oh, baby, the way you been licking Zior's ass, he'd let you jump into bed with your gigolo without saying a word.'

'You're absolutely repulsive, Archibald.'

'Up yours too, creeping Annie! What right have you to be so high and mighty, what have you ever done for the poor and the weak and the sick? Just make them sicker, that's all. You're sick yourself and what's more you make me sick. If ever there were a whited sepulchre, you're it.'

'Shut up, you're a heretic and a sadist. Putting up with you is mental torture, you are tearing me apart.'

'I can say just as much for you. I will add that your so called noble stature, your endless moral judgement, and the arrogant way of your British upbringing, not forgetting your very nature as an old bigot, is ruining my eternal rest.'

'Archie, if you only knew how much I hate you. When I was down on Earth, I disliked quite a lot of people, but by God, I would never have thought once dead I could hate someone as much as I despise you. It's incredible, if actually I could I would take your guts out.'

He wagged a finger at her: 'What a rotten thought, terribly surprising coming from someone who claims to be a good Christian.'

They glowered at each other for a long moment. At length he resumed: 'You know what Zior will do if we don't get rid of your precious banjo player? He'll keep us here for all eternity. We'll both be prisoners and it'll be your fault, smarty pants.'

'Eternity with you, I'd rather go straight to hell.'

'Be reasonable, Daisy. You know as well as I do that we can't force him to join up with his body. He's a free agent, just like we are free to work calmly together or scratch each other's eyes out.'

'If you are so clever,' she countered, 'what do you suggest? Maybe we should get married and adopt him.'

'Big joke! Adopting him might do something for your barren womb. Seriously, I believe we should be trying to find out why he is so obstinate.'

'It's evident enough. He won't go back because he doesn't want to be paralyzed for the rest of his life.'

Archie raised his bowler hat, scratched his head with his other hand, and lowered the bowler again.

'Maybe, maybe not. I suspect he simply wants to solve the mysteries of the hereafter.'

'Is that all?' she snorted.

'It's no laughing matter. He's done pretty well for himself so far. Treillet wasn't born yesterday. He's still here, he'll be dead tomorrow if he finds out those mysteries. Y'know, all it needs is a little charm on your part. Feed him some of your feminine charm and he'll be eating out of your hand. He'll see reason.'

'Why me?'

'Because you're a woman. Treillet seems to be fond of women. Try a striptease number on him. That should scare the wits out of him and send him back down at the speed of light.'

'Archie, you really are a cad. Even though I hate you, I will not lower myself to curse you.'

Treillet squatted in a far corner of the room with the white walls, wondering how long he'd been there. Time made no sense in the Centre, it seemed.

Bleakly he watched the hospital scene still on the screen opposite him. The twenty four hour clock in the intensive care room showed 7a.m. He recalled that his operation had terminated at 9p.m. the previous evening. Everything was quiet, and he supposed that even his Other Self was taking a rest. Bob gave a sigh that was half chuckle half snort.

Soon his colleagues and friends would start making enquiries, either phoning or calling in. With luck he would make the midday TV news, which pleased him as a prospect. Having regard to his controversial image, any publicity was good publicity.

He noticed a magazine left open on a table next to the bed, he couldn't tell which, perhaps Paris Match, perhaps a pop music magazine. He moved across and, on closer examination, saw colour photos of himself in action.

'Hey, you two,' he called out to Archie and Daisy. 'Come in and see this. See those pictures. That's me last week doing a show in Bordeaux.'

'Really? How interesting,' said Archie. 'Tell me, do you always perform sitting down?'

'Sure I do, the guitar gets heavy after a bit. Besides, I cradle it like I'm making love to a girl. It turns the fans on.'

'It would be better I should think if you moved around sometimes. Otherwise, it's like a charity number at an old folks' home.'

Mackenzie started jiving around and undulating his middle.

'See, a little momentum never hurt anyone. What you need in a show is action, things happening. Got to keep 'em interested.'

Archie threw his cane into the air and missed it when it came down. It clattered ignominiously to the floor.

Bob knew that his style had nothing to do with any of Michael Jackson's acts, but being criticized by a so called choreographer incapable of keeping his balance on a straight line, made him angry.

'Not my style at all,' said Bob.

Daisy gave a hoot: 'Well, at all events Archie now knows about the law of gravity. Watch those rheumatics, old trouper.'

'Let me tell the two of you, I know what the public goes for, after thirty years of choreographing on Broadway,' Archie growled.

'Thirty years in and out of brothels is more likely,' Daisy hastened to say.

'I worked hard for my living. Not everyone is born with an army of housemaids at their service.'

Daisy stuck her nose in the air.

'Now, Monsieur Treillet, I have to inform you that Zior, our director, has rejected your request for an extension of your stay at the Centre. So will you kindly leave for the hospital at once. Otherwise we shall have you removed by force,' said Daisy with the assurance of a bailiff handing notice to an insolvent tenant.

The voyager gave a twitch of his head: 'I refuse to travel one centimetre farther without adequate life insurance, stipulating that I won't stay bedridden, correctly signed and initialled by Zior.'

'Archibald, kindly make him understand.'

The American proferred him a condescending smile: 'Don't pay too much attention to her. She's suffering from post-menopausal anguish. I assume that it's your future state of health that's worrying you?'

'I'll be disabled. Perhaps mentally handicapped too.'

'They could be wrong. The human frame is very resilient. Doctors make mistakes like the rest of us with the difference that sometimes their mistakes can be deadly.'

'Dr. Koln is known for his infallible diagnoses,' Bob mumbled. 'I am prepared to go back provided you can guarantee that I shan't be debilitated. You said yourself a moment ago that I ought to move around when I perform my numbers. Come on, Archie, we're in the same business, an invalid artist wouldn't get a look-in. Let's say I'll be a weeny bit crippled, and that might even get me added support from the fans. So I'll meet you half way on the question.'

Archie and Daisy remained tight-lipped, and he went on: 'If you're worried about getting a reprimand from your superiors in the event that I make a claim, I'm even prepared to pay a quick trip to Lourdes.'

Still no reaction from the other two.

'God won't like it if you refuse me a helping hand.'

'This is no-man's land and you are still responsible for your actions, the good ones as well as the bad things,' warned Daisy.

Archie looked at the floor and Daisy stood rigid with her arms crossed.

'I see,' Bob sighed. 'We'll try it another way. I'd like something to write with, if it's not too much trouble. It's my future that's at stake. I have a right and a duty to defend my interests.'

'What's the writing stuff for?' Archie enquired.

'Since you won't say anything, neither will I.'

'Maybe you'd like a fax machine too?'

'Why not? And a guitar as well, so I can play you the Death March,' joked Bob, getting some fun at resisting them.

Archie looked Bob straight in the face, producing an egg timer from his pocket.

'Don't you have anything more appetizing for lunch than boiled eggs?' Bob swaggered.

'Death is staring you in the face, Bob, and I'm not joking this time. I'm going to start this timer in a moment, and when it has run out, you risk being clinically dead. Then, I will be very surprised to still find you so talkative. Daisy said the human soul fed on being nice to others.'

'Judging by her scrawny body, she looks like she has been fasting for eternity,' observed Bob.

Archie placed the timer on the floor next to the computer. A hush fell on the room, save for the almost imperceptible whisper of the first sand grains falling.

Daisy drifted through the wall, followed by her colleague.

'You'll never get away with this!' Bob shouted at them. 'I'll have the law on you, this is downright murder!'

Archie did a wobbly pirouette, staggered as he tried to keep his balance, and disappeared. His clumsiness irritated him a lot. Down on Earth, he had danced with the lightness of a Bolshoi star, feeling at home in classical or modern. In view of his permanent weightlessness at the Centre, his suppleness ought to have increased ten-fold, instead of which he seemed as stiff as a rusty step ladder. Daisy told him he was lucky Zior hadn't fitted him out with crutches, after his dissolute behaviour in New York.

So Bob was alone again with death just around the corner. Long may it remain so. He'd be clinically dead when the timer ran out, a vegetable powerless to fight for his own life. The prospect filled him with utter gloom. He'd be worse than homeless, a kind of stateless refugee stuck in the Centre for eternity perhaps, or heading for either Heaven or Hell. Agreed, he hadn't taken religion seriously so far, but when you were confronted with imminent mortality, you had to admit that there was a remote possibility that the theologians were right.

Bob had always found difficulty reasoning things out, he had never really learnt to think with the purpose of reaching a conclusion. He had always preferred the spontaneous way of overcoming obstacles, leapfrogging over facts that didn't suit him. For perhaps the first time ever, he strove to organize his mind, as he stared at the egg timer. But Bob was no Sherlock Holmes, he lacked the great detective's precision and rigour. All he knew was that, by some quirk or fissure in the cosmic mechanism, he had reached the edge of the hereafter unofficially, a place where the stream of life ran thin and small. He remembered his astronomer friend, and in a flash of wild hope wished he could contact him via the computer; since astronomers had trained minds, they understood how all those stupid stars came to be charging around in the firmament like some loose rugby scrum.

Yes, they knew the 'how', but even they didn't know the 'what for'.

If only he knew the object of the exercise, the meaning of creation, of life and what followed it …

More immediate questions tickled his brain. Who exactly were those idiots Archie and Daisy? What precisely was Zior's role in the great scheme of things? How did Zior relate to the divinity? Why didn't the Supreme Power, (their expression), intervene? How much time had he really got left to him?

He longed for some guardian angel, even God Himself, to come and stand right before him to help him picture the situation.

A born optimist, Treillet sensed that his Other Self was scoring points as the seconds went by, sapping his confidence in a moment of anguish such as all humans suffer at times of crisis.

Treillet didn't know it, but the mirror in the room was two-way. Daisy watched him through it now. Archie was at his desk, feet up as usual.

'All I can say is your egg timer trick had better work,' she growled. 'If it doesn't you'd better come up with something or the eggs will crack.'

Mackenzie waved a hand nonchalantly: 'There's no need to preach at me. Especially as you seem to be egg-bound yourself. What happened to your woman's intuition? Why can't you think up something? Don't worry, I'll take him by surprise and surprise you too.'

'Nothing you can do would surprise me any more. You've given me too many shocks already.'

Archie's problem was that certain principles had to be obeyed at the Universal Selection Centre. Not principles of an earthly kind such as gentlemanly codes of conduct, fair play, consideration for others and so on, but those to do with infinite universal love and forgiveness. Therein lay the difficulty. For example, it was hard to see how anyone in their right mind could love and forgive a harridan like Lady Daisy. On the other hand, if that was the way he could obtain spiritual promotion and achieve a higher level of excellence, he'd have a shot at it.

Mackenzie had been presented with a moral dilemma the moment he reached the Centre. Zior had asked him outright: 'What have you done with your life?' As if Zior didn't know; obviously it had been a rhetorical question. Archie's instinct had been to tell him to mind his own business. But wiser counsel prevailed, he recalled a line by the comedian Bob Hope: 'Brave men run in my family'.

Supposing, he told himself, that the Supreme Power actually cared about him, which would have been a rather nice thing for Zior to have said. Bearing in mind his eventful existence over the years, Archie didn't know where to start sorting out his conscience; that called for an expertise that he had never acquired. It was a bit like going back to school, passing exams one after the other, or akin to going through a commando course in the army.

Daisy had been asked the same question, and it had knocked the wind out of her. She had told Archie that surely the Almighty knew about her blameless life as a Christian, the battles she had never lost against the seven capital sins, her loyalty to the high standards laid down in scripture and the prayer book, not forgetting her immense service to the British throne, the Queen being the head of the Church of England. She also told Archie that, when she herself failed to be accepted on face value, it was surprising that Zior should be so lenient with Archie. It vexed her, furthermore, that she had to waste time running the Centre's office for special cases, as if she needed to earn her keep in the after-life, whereas in her opinion she'd more than earned her place already in the top echelons.

Archibald's arrival as her subordinate was the last straw. Obviously a serious error had been made by someone, for she certainly didn't deserve that additional crown of thorns. Errare humanum est, persistere diabolicum! she had been fond of quoting when on Earth. By depriving her of her own spiritual advancement, Zior no doubt expected her to teach her American colleague right from wrong, but it was a thankless labour. Someone had blundered, that was certain.

As she continued scrutinizing Treillet, Mackenzie rose from his recumbent posture to dance up and down the white line separating the two halves of their office, arms outstretched like a tightrope walker. Daisy at last moved away from the two-way mirror and hunched over her prayer stool. Depressed by the disastrous consequences of the rebellious Treillet, Daisy gave herself blows on the chest with the rage of a flagellating nun.

In a gesture of compassion, Archie laid a hand on his colleague's shoulder. Daisy straightened with the speed of a rattlesnake whose tail had been stepped on by a careless jogger.

'Touch me not,' she hissed through her teeth. 'You know how I hate the very idea of a man's dirty hands on me. You are in my territory, leave me alone.'

Mackenzie complied with the remark: 'Daisy, my sweet, you'll never make progress until you learn humility.'

'Huh, progress! All you want to do is drag me down to your level, tarnishing my very soul. You are my occasion of sin.'

'You mean you want a roll in the hay?'

'I didn't say an occasion for sin. Your knowledge of moral teaching is appalling.'

'Don't blame me for your hang-ups, we never met on Earth and you can't hold me responsible. Why don't you tell me exactly what happened? Come on, let it all hang out. Confession is good for the soul.'

Daisy sniffed. 'Confession! That Romish hypocrisy! Wiping the slate clean so that one can get up to mischief again.'

'You're hiding something. You must have had some unfortunate experience. Someone did something to you, it's not natural for you to be so afraid of men. Let me help you find peace of mind.'

'Since when has my peace of mind concerned you? Why do you have to reduce everything to s-e-x? It is all so trivial and bestial.'

'Because I believe that your big problem lies there. Will you dare to say otherwise? We're given our bodies to enjoy. Sperm is the spice of life!'

'That's your opinion. Stop ogling me. I really can't discuss the subject. You'd only laugh at me. You just want a cheap thrill, you Peeping Tom!'

'Not at all, I give you my word. I take sex seriously. I won't laugh.'

'Cross your heart and tell no lies.'

'Daisy, as a man of honour, I swear I won't laugh at you.'

'Men have no honour. Swear on the head of the Supreme Power, I'll accept that.'

Until now, Makenzie had not been very respectful of higher authority but adopting blasphemy seemed to him a hazardous road. Archie solemnly traced a cross on his chest with a thumb.

'All right, I swear on the head of you know Whom that I won't laugh at you,' he said without much conviction.

Daisy shut her eyes, took a deep breath and rose from the prayer stool to pace the room with clutched hands.

'When I was still a pimply teenager I lost my parents in a shipwreck in the Bermuda Triangle, and I went to live with my grandparents in their Sussex manor house. One Christmas Eve as I was sitting in the drawing room on my own looking at the lights and tinsel on the Christmas tree, the duke, my grandfather, came in dressed as Santa Claus. I was alone with him. My grandmother, the duchess, was away doing things with the gardener.'

'Emulating Lady Chatterley.'

'Archie! Anyway, he approached me slowly, rather like some cheeky animal playing a game of sorts, as I supposed. He was grinning and making his eyes big. I was only thirteen at the time. I really didn't know what to think about his attitude. If he wanted to play the fool I thought I ought to humour him and do something appropriate. So I too began jumping about and twirling around rather like a ballet dancer. Of course my dress flared out and I noticed that he was starting to breathe hard, panting, with his eyes rivetted on my legs.'

'Do go on.'

'Well, I saw him gather the hem of his cloak and – and ...'

'And what Daisy?'

'I can't say it,' moaned Daisy, putting her hands to her face and blushing.

'You must.'

'I wasn't afraid at first. He was an eminent personage, decorated by the Queen Mother for his role in World War II, he had beaten General Rommel's highest ranking officer in a camel race through the Sahara desert.

'That's a hell of a performance,' Archie said in wonder.

'He pulled the cloak right up to his waist and tucked the cloak into his belt, and he had nothing on underneath. And then I saw it, his thingy dangling there, swaying about. It was enormous, sticking out at me.'

'His thingy.'

'Yes, his p-penis. He had a penis.'

'No doubt.'

'It was all pink and shiny.'

'He'd washed it for the festive season.'

'Not at all. No, it was not a normal one.'

'So you'd seen a normal one before?'

'Stop interrupting. It was like a long balloon, and it swung about.'

'But it didn't burst.'

'No, it was made of plastic!'

Daisy paused for effect. Archie put a hand to his brow. She looked at him miserably.

'It sounds cheap to me, wouldn't be surprised if that thingy was made in Taiwan.'

'You said you wouldn't make jokes.'

'Some joke, a plastic popgun, for crying out loud. Your grandpa sounds really kinky. So what happened next? Do go on, I'm all ears.'

'Oh dear, this is awful.'

'But highly intriguing. The plot thickens.'

'He began rubbing it,' she said hurriedly. 'And he came at me and pulled my dress up, and pulled down my knickers. You can imagine what he tried to do next.'

'He went after the promised land!'

'At that very minute God took mercy on me; he was stricken with a fatal heart attack.'

As the tears streamed down on her face, she sobbed: 'It was horrid.'

'I'm flabbergasted,' said Archie. 'What a dirty old duke. Plastic thingy, for chrissakes.'

He took her arm and mumbled a few words of sympathy.

'Now you understand,' Daisy squeaked. 'Since that incident I have always refused to have anything whatever to do with men, especially in the physical sense. That is why I want you to leave me alone, and please don't mention s-e-x again. In any case, you are as much a pervert as he was. All men are beastly.'

'That, Daisy, is the generalization of the century,' Mackenzie concluded. 'Might make a good title for a movie, though. A blue movie for lesbians.'

Archie eyed Daisy for an instant to see if he had touched a sensitive point. But Daisy merely shooed him back to his desk and his crossword puzzle. She knelt again to her endless prayers. If she had a prediliction for her own gender, she was hiding it well, Archie had to admit.

Some time later, Archie and Daisy were again spying on their voyager through the two-way mirror. On the floor of the white-walled room lay a multicoloured banner with the message 'L-S-F'. The day will come when mortals and immortals shall be one with the Divine Light.'

'Did you put that there?' her ladyship demanded.

'Yep,' replied Archie, as Treillet woke up from a snooze, rubbed his eyes and blinked on seeing the banner.

'Now you've done it, Archibald, you've burned our boats. Angels and ministers of grace defend us. I suppose this is the surprise you promised. You realize you've given him the one thing he should never have. The sacred code. Oh, calamity!'

'Ah, there's beauty to my scheme. If he ever gets to decipher the code, he'll never be able to use it. He'll toddle off with the formula, he'll be off our hands, but it'll be no use to him.'

'But you've messed everything up for us. If he does get to decipher it, we shall have eternal rest snatched from under our noses. We might even be damned for eternity. Do something quick, I beseech you, or the game's up for both of us.'

'You sound like Pontius Pilate. You've given in.'

'What! Don't you compare me to that tight-arse, if you'll excuse the expression.'

'I use it myself quite often,' Archie returned with a glare. 'Calm down, we have plenty of time.'

'The damage is done, you fool.'

Archie squared his shoulders: 'You don't imagine I'd let him pull a fast one on me. Not on your sweet fanny. He'll fall for this, you'll see.'

'Your gutter language gets worse. He will see through your trick, like he always does. We're stuck with him now.'

She grabbed her prayer book and began flicking through the pages, looking for an appropriate response.

Archie continued observing the voyager, who was mouthing the letters L-S-F, trying to figure them out.

Supposing, Bob cogitated, that the Supreme Power had made a monkey out of us all with his Creation. Nature itself explained nothing – all those tigers and birds of prey and sharks tearing one another to pieces, all those natural disasters and epidemics. And man was as bad as they were. If homo sapiens really were the greatest achievement in the universe, and the best the Creator could do, then it was about time He thought again. Man was the worst killer of them all, any ecologist would tell you. Bob reckoned that if he were the Creator he'd scrap the whole silly project and start again from scratch. God probably created woman to make up for his mistake in creating man. And to cap it all, sent his Son in a final wild bid to put things right. Tough luck on J.C. – the biggest fall guy of them all!

Treillet emitted a cynical laugh. The theologians hadn't thought it through. Man was supposed to be loaded down with Original Sin, and they invented Lucifer as an easy way for God to pass the buck. Far better to have engineered the process correctly in the Great Design Office instead of resorting to makeshift repairs later. Original Sin, what rubbish! Tax deducted at source, more likely. When he next saw Archie and Daisy he'd give them a piece of his mind. And if Lady Daisy tried to big-mouth him with her preaching and her other nonsense, he'd tell her to contact his Other Self. Let them argue it all out between them. He wasn't going to waste his time on a lot of metaphysics and whatnot.

Mackenzie continued watching Treillet. He reasoned that if he divulged the meaning of the code to the voyager, the poor guy would never be able to apply it. Treillet was clearly a man who preferred action to solving riddles.

He passed through the wall and confronted Bob. Daisy feared the worst, and decided there and then to report the whole matter of the banner to Zior.

To her horror she heard Archie tell Treillet: 'L-S-F means Love-Serenity-Faith. These three make up the secret way to immortality.'

'Well, why didn't you say so in the first place? This changes everything,' the Frenchman cried out.

'There wasn't much point,' Archie shrugged, 'since you will never be able to carry it out. Throughout history a few exceptionally gifted people – so called saints, artists, statesmen, whatever – have tried to apply the L-S-F formula so as to achieve immortality. Nobody has ever succeeded, they have at best merely gained the tag "immortal" in the eyes of human posterity. They all without exception had doubts, and those doubts were fatal. They were and still are human beings and nothing better.'

Archie thought: 'Bob of all people is not going to be any different. He can write songs and sing them until he's blue in the face, but it won't improve his lot. Everyone from Adam and Eve onward has had an Other Self, and he has one too, as he is well aware. This being so, he might as well join up with his body again. His ULM accident will have no consequences.' 'You won't be disabled and mentally handicapped,' Archie declared, looking him straight in the eyes, 'You will be as fit as a fiddle and I wouldn't be surprised if you live to be 100, hale and hearty into the bargain, although I have no accurate information on that last point.'

Archie was quite pleased at his throwaway line. It made the rest of his story more credible. He went on to tell his listener to forget and forgive his Other Self, and never look back. Mackenzie told him not to worry about immortality. To think in terms of eternal rest and make the most of his earthly chances. The business of going through life was complicated enough, so there was no need to wear his brain out with a lot of speculation about immortality and the after-life.

Archie strove to conceal his excitement. His arguments were scoring. Behind his frivolous exterior, he was a perceptive fellow, he knew that Bob was an impulsive sort, that he would go for the immediate prize of a happy life on Earth. His career so far had shown that, and his awkward attitude since arriving at the Centre had confirmed it. Archie had played on his naive and impetuous nature. For his own good, Treillet's own good.

'I'm inclined to agree with you,' Bob smiled guardedly, not wishing to show that he'd accepted Archie's views hook, line and sinker. 'Decent of you to spell it out this way, I'm very grateful to you. We French have a reputation for complicating the simplest things, you must excuse us. Shake a paw, Archie old bean.'

Mackenzie was delighted, the poor sap was even making excuses for himself. They shook hands, and on an impulse Bob flung his arms around Archie, giving him a kiss on each cheek, French style.

As they separated, Bob told him that when he got back down there, he'd like to set up a kind of universal brotherhood society, a peace on earth thing. They might even run it together, he on Earth, and Archie up here. As Bob was having trouble thinking up a name, Archie suggested he call it the Union for Renovating the Planet – URP for short. That should bring the customers in. Bob offered Archie the post of honorary president.

Before leaving the voyager, Mackenzie handed him an envelope, asking him to deliver it personally to the producer of Manhattan Follies. He rolled up the banner, gave Bob a final pat on the back, and disappeared.

Instantly, all the lights of the computer went out, and Bob stood in complete silence, unsure of what he had done, wondering what would happen next.

Back in his office, the one-time Broadway showman resumed his seat at his desk after pulling out the computer plug.

He set to musing about his present woes, and especially about the lack of attractive female company at the Centre.

How his tired old eyes would brighten if Ingrid Bergman walked in and tapped him on the shoulder, or Bette Davis or the great Marilyn Monroe herself. Perhaps they were somewhere around, but Zior was keeping them out of sight.

Archie realized that Zior had paired him up with Daisy as a penance for his earthly misconduct.

He'd been obliged to work hard at his career. His slight pot belly and chubby cheeks were against him, and his flat feet had forced him to seek new pastures as a choreographer. Even so he was popular with the girls due to his cheerful nature, his evident vitality and the wisecracks that sprang from his lips like candyfloss from a machine.

Mackenzie had another additional appeal, he listened to the girls' troubles and could always be relied on for a kind word of advice and sympathy.

His amorous advances usually began as a candlelight meal for two cooked by himself with the same skill as he intended to show in the boudoir. He chose his wines with care and made sure his guest's glass was always two-thirds filled. The rest was a piece of cake, beginning around 11p.m. when the object of his desire was invariably too muzzy with the fruit of the vine, his compliments and promises to resist his busy fingers. In Archie Mackenzie, Casanova had a successor worthy of the name. He was also a connoisseur of three-sided sessions, car-key parties, strip poker and gentle flagellation in the service of jaded wives eager for daring new experiments. Despite his obsession with carnal pleasures, Mackenzie had a golden rule, viz, that his conquests must be aged between sixteen and fifty. Too young was asking for complications in court; as to the upper limit, he was in no need of the older woman.

As a young man earning pocket money by doing a little gardening, he had once seduced the lady of the house, her daughter and the Polish nanny all in one week and the man of the house sent him away without payment of any kind. He had never repeated that type of exercise.

In order to get his way, he many times promised marriage but no woman ever got him within miles of the altar. As proof of his success he used to ask for, and always obtained, an article of clothing from his partner, and on his death the family discovered a collection at his place of nearly 2,000 pairs of panties, along with a file in alphabetical order listing his victims' names, their ratings one to five, dates and annotations. These were for him to look back on in his riper years. He pictured himself on the veranda of his future Hollywood ranch house, reminiscing in a rocking chair, probably with an inflatable doll by his side.

He created a good deal of drama in the years of his prime, several women having taken an overdose of pills, five others entering homes for the mentally ill, and some twins going into a convent in an odour of post-coital sanctity.

When he died suddenly on the stage during the dress rehearsal for Manhattan Follies, the funeral was attended by several dozen ladies who came to gloat. The timing of his death when his greatest (and only) stage triumph was imminent, continued to irritate him far into the after-life.

His death was triggered to some extent by a young lady who gained the top award of the dance academy. She danced with exquisite beauty and took the lead role in the show. Suddenly, as the curtain was about to go up, she refused point blank to go on stage. This deliberate act of sabotage was to damn him for ever on Broadway.

The explanation was to be found some twenty years earlier when Archie fell violently in love with a girl student who found she was pregnant. Mackenzie however had no intention of being trapped, and walked out on her, advising her to have an abortion. The girl preferred to keep the child, but never got over the event, entering a clinic for the mentally handicapped where she languished for several years.

When the student died, her daughter the dancer learned who the father was. That Archie Mackenzie, her own father, should have abandoned her in this cowardly fashion, shook her to the core. Her contempt and hatred developed into an obsession and she vowed to make him pay for his despicable treatment of her mother.

When the dancer refused to go on stage on that opening night, Mackenzie collapsed. He had known deep down that, one day, he would suffer as a result of his womanizing, but he'd never imagined that he would fall victim to his own child. He had never rejected the idea of marriage and having a family, but he feared the reaction of his wife when she was confronted with his infidelity. Divorce would inevitably have resulted, and their offspring would have paid the consequences for sure.

However that may be, the Divine Powers had kept their views to themselves. But from the instant of his death, his daughter had become the most important person in his thoughts. His love for her exceeded all his other loves, which he believed moreover was in keeping with the divine principles.

Manhattan Follies opened later, the media and the public being more interested in the circumstances surrounding his demise than in the quality or otherwise of the production. He was cut down at the pinnacle of his success, he told himself, except that he never reached the pinnacle.

Lady Daisy was equally frustrated at the Centre, though for totally different reasons. She who had spent her life improving the behaviour of others, wondered why she was stuck with someone as reprehensible as Archibald Mackenzie.

She had implored Zior to relieve her of the burden, prayed to the Almighty to bear in mind her life's devotion to the Anglican church and to take this bitter chalice from her lips. To no avail. Repeatedly she looked back over the story of her trudge through life to see if there were a crack in the edifice, but found only a record of impeccable morality and perfect submission, if not to the divine will, at least to the deity's general instructions. Surely, she contended, it would be hard indeed to find a worthier task on Earth than serving and preserving the British throne. What would they have done without her at the palace? She had commanded the staff there with a diligence so thorough that none of them had managed to exceed her own length of service. Proof enough that she was the right person for the job. Whenever a fork or napkin was out of place, a wig askew or a sheet unaired, the culprit was dismissed without further debate. Her basic rule was that the palace staff should, in the dying embers of the century, be as efficient and obsequious as their forerunners in 1901. This may indeed be a decadent epoch, but its influence must never be allowed within the royal gates. Her whole being had been bound up with the history of the British monarchy since Alfred the Great (died 899) and she resented having Archibald the Degenerate thrust upon her as consort. He was past saving, she asserted.

Naturally, with her impregnable principles, she spent half her nights thinking up punishments for the wrongdoers of the coming day. Sometimes she fell to dreaming that she herself was the lawful crowned queen. To tell the truth, she sincerely believed that she'd make a better go of things, and would stride along the corridors of power in her Victorian crinoline, a bargain at a Sotheby's auction, bowing to imaginary courtiers, footmen, maidservants, prime ministers and other menials, glancing at priceless paintings of war and peace treaties, checking up on the Empire and generally organizing the realm and its dominions across the seas. On these occasions, watched with misgiving by the security staff, she would stop by Queen Victoria's old bedroom, easing herself into a gilded armchair to face the royal bed where Victoria Regina and her consort Albert discussed where to send the next day's gunboat before putting the light out. How happy and glorious the couple must have been. Daisy vowed that if ever she had a husband, dreadful thought, she would call him Albert, even if his name were John.

Queen Victoria was her heroine. She admired her pre-eminence, her ability to control allies as well as enemies, her feminine wiles which she employed to divide and rule, her use of the stick rather than the carrot. Victoria would have made short work of Oliver Cromwell Esquire, that wart-covered upstart and regicide who came within an ace of ruining the country while setting the stage for the worst calamity in world history, the French Revolution.

Lady Daisy had a particular dislike of the popular press, owing to their story-telling about the lesser royals. 'Lies all lies!' she would howl whenever a new scandal broke. She was sure these tales were leaked by members of her staff, and would arrange for the suspects to be bugged and phone-tapped like Bolshevik spies. If proof were unobtainable she would readily provide suitable evidence against them herself and the supposed leaker would be dismissed with ignominy. Unfortunately the detested media used this event to create a further outcry, wanting to know how many other moles there were close to the monarchy, demanding who controlled the moles.

Her ladyship was known to the personnel as The Tyrannosaurus and she had no allies among her underlings. Late one evening when a drunken chauffeur bowled her over on her way back from the kennels where she kept her rottweiler hound, the entire staff gathered round to make sure she was dead.

Daisy was mortified, on arrival at the Centre, to discover that the authorities could tell her nothing about the arrangements for her funeral.

For years previously she had hoped, not only that the service would be presided over by His Grace the Archbishop of Canterbury in person, but also that the Houses of Lords and Commons would assemble in unity for a minute's silence. Instead of which the Archbishop the day after her death saw fit to leave by plane for a fishing trip in New Zealand, the Commons dealt with the second reading of the Education Reform Bill Mark 24 B, and the Lords spent the day discussing the impending closure of a railway halt for grouse shooters somewhere in Scotland.

One is never properly appreciated, she sighed as she took possession of her Second Empire desk.

Happy as a sandboy, the voyager set out on the return journey through the dimly lit tunnel.

This time there were no alligators or other strange creatures and he skipped along doing the twist, singing his heart out to words of his own invention:

We don't know where we're going,
And there's no way of knowing,
But the future is a-glowing, I'm not telling no lies.
We don't need no choir,
We're just aiming higher,
To set the world on fire, and we'll all get a prize.

From now on his life would have real meaning, he had found his true self at last and had a clear vocation. He would set up the Union for Renovating the Planet (URP), open to all men and women of all races, all political persuasions and all religious aspirations.

The scheme as he sketched it out made him feel quite heady. It was action at last, nothing less than a world-wide Marshall Plan but infinitely more ambitious. And why not? The Universe was big enough for the Supreme Power to let him save the tiny Planet Earth. Treillet was struck by the logic of his project. Since the clerics, monarchs, trade unionists, scholars and the rest of the self-styled elite had made such a mess of the economy and society, a more imaginative approach was needed, they should step aside for the musicians. Let those lead who could. Music, he argued, knew no frontiers. The 200-year-old slogan Liberty, Equality, Fraternity was no longer enough, it had seen its moment of glory, but now the time had come to set up a world community having neither God nor masters, to quote the familiar anarchist rallying cry. Away with apathy, welcome joy! The whole of mankind would feel a great burden of moroseness lifted from its shoulders.

Admittedly his ideas needed a little tidying up, but the framework was in place. In practice he would need to build the brave new world with subtlety, it was no good mounting a frontal attack against the powers of reaction, the enormous magma of those who doubt and are afraid to move forward. Better to go quietly at first, gathering a band of loyal disciples from the four corners of the globe. Then surprise everyone with the revolution to end all revolutions, in one fell swoop.

A worm of doubt entered his soul. Would the mass of the people go along with him, did they want change of this dimension, were they even interested in change at all? He fancied he heard Daisy's stern voice echoing along the tunnel walls, trying to sabotage his plan. Or perhaps it was Archie with a last-minute message.

His stomach turned over when the truth impinged itself on his mind; his Other Self was back!

If his Other Self were staging a counter-attack before the struggle had even begun, it could mean that the fellow was afraid he would succeed. Mind you, he mustn't imagine things, he might be hearing voices like Joan of Arc had. The Maid of Orleans had taken up her sword with disastrous consequences, her burning faith had ended with burning toes. He meant to be smarter and make sure of what those voices were telling him.

His Other Self was evidently trying to re-establish contact, and the motive was to distract him from the URP project. Of course, his long-time adversary was a wet blanket, a spoilsport by his very nature. Archie had assured him that he would recover and be as right as rain in no time, but he had produced no actual evidence to back this up, there was only his word to go on.

At this point a huge two-headed dragon leapt out and barred his passage, breathing fire, Thinking quickly, he yelled the three-letter code L-S-F. To no avail, he was engulfed in flames in a matter of seconds. So much for Love-Serenity-Faith.

Treillet spun round and hurtled back towards the Centre, as more horrific creatures joined the dragon, chasing him like a pack of raging dogs.

He emerged from the tunnel and, as previously, a great light inundated the upper entrance. The monsters stayed inside, yowling and snarling, baring their fangs.

Treillet fought to steady his breathing. Mackenzie had warned him against doubt. It was an old trick by priests and such who nattered about faith, and he had been daft enough to let himself be caught out. Mackenzie had told him last time that the beasts he encountered were the product of his subconscious and he had failed to control it. Faith might move mountains, but apparently it couldn't get a man through a measly tunnel.

Bob stood miserably wondering what was to become of him. He also wondered if he might not be part of the snivelling magma that opposed change.

4

From the safety of her prayer stool, Daisy glowered at Archie through half-closed eyes. This time she really would report his disgraceful performance to Zior.

Not only had the imbecile revealed the secret code for obtaining immortality, he had sent their visitor off through the tunnel with false hopes, only to have him return to the Centre intent on vengeance. They were worse off than ever, Mackenzie had achieved nothing and laid the foundations for a devastating battle of wills.

Zior must be informed, that was obvious. She would turn the tables on Archibald, stressing that only the severest punishment was good enough for him.

Daisy watched Treillet through the two-way mirror as he paced furiously back and forth in the computer room by himself, glancing ominously at the mirror now and again from his side of the wall.

'Only Zior can deal with this new situation,' she said levelly.

'Things are getting complicated. We have too many balls up in the air,' Archie admitted.

'And whose silly fault is that? You knew perfectly well that humans don't have the ability to apply the L-S-F formula.'

'So what's the beef? All I wanted to do was to get him off our hands and back with his body. How was I to know he'd have second thoughts half way through the tunnel? He was fully convinced when he left here.'

Mackenzie jabbed a hole in the wall with his cane and went through, followed by Lady Daisy.

Treillet immediately bounded forward, landing an uppercut to Archie's jaw.

'Stop that this minute!' Daisy ordered. 'Where do you think you are, in some Texas saloon? My colleague hasn't played fair with you, but all forms of violence are strictly prohibited at the Centre. Next time you hit him, I will hit you back.'

Daisy shook her fists at Treillet. Archie's jaw dropped, he was amazed to find that she was on his side for once.

'You goddam liar, Mackenzie,' said Bob. 'I'm only sorry you can't feel anything physically or I would tear you apart.'

'I simply forgot to tell you a few details,' the other said.

'You're still telling lies. Don't worry, Lady Daisy, I'll keep my fists to myself, I wouldn't demean myself by knocking the daylights out of him.'

From his pocket the disappointed traveller drew the envelope Archie had handed him. He tore it into little bits, went to the door and threw the bits in the tunnel.

'What was in that envelope?' Daisy demanded.

'Oh nothing, nothing at all,' Mackenzie said, clearing his throat.

'You're lying again.'

'It was only a few notes for my biography.'

'Which, I suppose, will be called Mackenzie's Folly. You really are off your rocker. I've always known you are not right in the head, and I'm only surprised that Zior doesn't realize it.'

Bob kept trying to halt this tirade, but she turned to him.

'As for you, Monsieur Treillet, I always knew one couldn't trust the French. Let's have no more nonsense now, you must obey our rules and not your own.'

'I formally request a personal interview with Zior,' the musician said.

'He never grants interviews to voyagers, even less to voyagers like yourself.'

'Well it's about time he did. I demand to see him.'

A voice with an electronic timbre resounded in the white-walled room. Daisy sprang to attention. She glanced at Archie to see if it was him doing another imitation, then saw that it wasn't.

'This is Zior,' the voice droned. 'First, I shall make no exception and will not see Treillet. Secondly, if Treillet means to stay here that's his and your problem. Thirdly, Mackenzie and Lady Daisy are forthwith suspended from duty, pending decisions as to their future from the Divine Light.'

Daisy began trembling. 'When will that be?' she asked.

'In due course.'

Archie broke in: 'Why not send Daisy on a refresher course? She looks like she needs one.'

'You be careful,' Zior told him. 'Or you'll need to check the small print on your fire insurance.'

Zior's warning message ended with a click. The three listeners were silent for a moment. Bob couldn't believe that he'd missed the opportunity of talking directly to Zior. His Other Self had probably stopped him, he reckoned.

Archie gave a nervous laugh. 'That's clear enough, anyway. We'd better have a general cease-fire while we're waiting for the Divine Light to get switched on.'

'How can you joke at a time like this? And don't be disrespectful to authority,' Daisy scolded.

The ex-choreographer stepped forward and extended his arms towards Treillet. 'All right, I admit I made a fool out of you. If we can't bury the hatchet, let's at least smoke the peace pipe. The ways things are going, I'll be giving off some smoke soon. I'm headed for the eternal barbecue, with Daisy on my tail, it seems. You might come out of this a lot better, Bob.'

Daisy had her hands over her face, she was crying hot tears.

'Hey what's with you?' Archie said. 'The Big Chief might let you go off to Saint-Tropez with Bob. Wouldn't mind a trip there myself, Madame Bardot might let me play with her teddy bears or something. Come on, honey, you ain't no Mary Magdalene.'

'Do stop trying to be funny,' Daisy wailed. 'It may help you, but it doesn't help me.'

Treillet had a suggestion:

'They must have some court of appeal here. Maybe we could set up a peoples' court. Don't cry Lady Daisy, we'll find a way.'

'Let her cry,' Archie said. 'She might be more charitable to others from now on, and it'll do her good.'

Rubbing her eyes, Daisy sobbed her way back to her quarters, lamenting: 'That it should come to this, after all I've done. I have never been dismissed before. What will become of me?'

'You could apply to the industrial court, if there is one,' Bob said helpfully. But Daisy had left already.

Archie turned to Bob: 'If I were you I'd try that tunnel again. There's a distinct smell of sulphur around here. I reckon you'll get through if you really mean to.'

'You don't really believe all that hellfire stuff,' Bob laughed. 'That's for the credulous. It smells to me more like opium than sulphur. Zior is simply trying to scare the pants off us all. He's bluffing.'

'I hope you're right. I'll tell you this much, I'm so bored here, I can't wait to hear what he has to say.'

'Let's be practical. The situation is explosive.'

'You can say that again. Any ideas?' Archie put to him.

'The Supreme Power, or whatever it is, is supposed to be all-forgiving. That's the theory, and if it's true then nobody's going to finish up in the fiery furnace. It would be against His principles. And besides, that would be admitting that He drew a few dud cards. His reputation wouldn't stand it. Mind you, there's bound to be some real sons of bitches here and there, mindless bastards who throw concrete onto motorways, self-centred men in high office who put their own interests above those of the nation, people who murder old ladies. I wouldn't be suprised if your Supreme Power makes the really nasty specimens just disappear completely.'

'Turns them into nothing, you mean? That's ridiculous.'

'Not really. They'll never do any good anywhere. Why waste time on them?'

Archie reflected. 'All the same, you can't deny that my prospects for rising higher in the spiritual life have gone up in smoke. You heard what Zior said about fire insurance.'

'Yeah. But maybe he's an even bigger liar than you are. That could be his little joke. If the Big Boss created the Universe and put people in it, why does He allow it to go mouldy? This business about Evil entering the world doesn't hold water; allowing Evil to exist is incitement to crime, which is a punishable offence, He'd be an accomplice, a guilty party Himself.'

Archie removed his bowler and scratched his head. 'Now you got me mixed up, and no mistake. Nothing makes any sense.'

'Exactly.'

'Exactly what?'

'There is no hellfire. Otherwise we're dealing with a mafia boss instead of a loving one.'

Mackenzie put up a hand. 'Hold it there, buddy. I only hope Zior hasn't bugged this room. It's one thing to jeer at old Daisy, but we can't accuse the Supreme Power of deliberately sowing Evil. We'd never get away with that. We are free to do Good or Evil, we can be guilty too. We're none of us clean as newborn babes. If I were you, I'd think twice about all that. Your undesirable presence here doesn't give you spiritual immunity.'

Treillet gave a shrug. 'I'm only thinking aloud, trying to work things out. People talk a lot about free will, but free expression is more important, to my way of thinking.'

'Hm. And I'm thinking you've caused enough trouble already up here. Let's leave it there, pal. I still don't trust Zior, that's all I know.'

Mackenzie uttered a snort and continued: 'We're getting too serious. Say, did you ever hear about the man who came home from the airport late one night to find his wife lying naked on the bed and a cigar still smoking in the ashtray next to the bed? "Where's this cigar come from?", he shouted. And a deep voice growled from under the bed. "Cuba, signor!"'

'Good story,' Bob agreed. 'But suppose I did manage to use the immortality formula and spread Love-Serenity-Faith all over the world. That'd be something worthwhile.'

Archie shook his head, visibly amused by the innocence of the voyager.

'You're a nice fellow, Bob. Even so, let me remind you that no human being has ever managed to make it work. So don't count on it yourself, you haven't been able to get through the tunnel. And you know why? You had doubts, my friend, huge doubts that made you fly into a panic and the doubts pulled the rug from under you. Even if you spent the rest of your life trying L-S-F, you wouldn't reach first base. Get that into your skull.'

'I'd like to try.'

'You're playing with fire, but I like your pluck. Pity we never met up down there, we'd have made a great double act. I'd have introduced you to some of the most gorgeous girls in the good old U.S.A. But certainly not to my daughter.'

'Why? What's wrong with her?'

'She ran out on me, and that's how I kicked the bucket pronto.'

He pulled a photo of her from his pocket. 'Cute ain't she?'

'Sure is. Doesn't look a bit like you!'

'And you're no Elvis Presley either. Just to think that I didn't live to see the opening night of Manhattan Follies. There was no justice in that world. She was fantastic, my daughter, danced like a fairy, and I don't mean a Californian fairy.'

'You'd have made a fortune from the show?'

'Possibly. Shucks, the past is the past, the curtain ran down as far as I am concerned. You're still in the game, though, and success may still come your way. Keep at it, Bob, remember Beethoven, he was a success even when he was deaf and blind. There's a genius for you! I'll be going, got to tidy up my desk. Daisy and I are only suspended from duty, but we may well have to quit for good.'

Mackenzie whizzed off through the wall. Moments later the opening of Beethoven's fifth symphony boomed out.

Beneath his cool exterior, Archie worried about his future in the hereafter. Bob might be right, maybe the Supreme Power dare not abandon incurable sinners. Even so, Archie did not intend to lick Zior's boots like Daisy did in order to win His mercy.

Bob Treillet began beating time to the symphony, but gave up after a few phrases. Obviously, Archie had switched the music on in another ploy to ease him back into the tunnel. He wasn't fooled by that, nobody in their right senses would compare his own efforts to the works of the great master of the German romantic tradition.

Strolling over to the computer, he again summoned up the scene in the hospital intensive care unit. He watched Emerald put some wild flowers in a vase by his bed. She sat on the edge of the bed, taking his hands and blowing onto the cold palms.

Unknown to Bob, the Eurasian had paid a short visit to his home that day, a local woman letting her in. Emerald had by now read, heard and seen the media coverage of Treillet's accident and operation, but had difficulty sorting out the facts from the fiction. She had gone to his cottage in the hope of learning more about her patient and the way he lived. Prior to the accident, Treillet had been simply another showbiz personality to her, but she was intrigued now that their paths had crossed.

The converted cottage surprised her with its ultra-modern furniture in some sort of hi-tech material, its pearly moonstone lamps, the startling surrealist paintings and multicoloured floor tiles. She had expected something more traditional in a place that must have dated back well over 100 years. Monsieur Treillet was a man with advanced tastes, and she wasn't sure she felt comfortable with them.

The girl studied the labels on the cassettes of his songs: Urchins of War, Contempt of Court, Revolution Now, Failures of The System, Death to My Other Half. The labels were handwritten, which seemed to indicate that the cassettes contained unpublished numbers. The young lady asked to hear some extracts, and the woman with her obliged. The songs were mostly to do with the sins of the Western capitalist economy. But Death to My Other Half was different. It began with the words:

I'm a soul in combat gear,
Fighting off my Other Half,
He said he was my brother,
But he stabbed me in the back.
Say your prayers false brother
I'm going to throw you away up there. . .

The woman told Emerald it was uncanny how the song fitted in with the ULM crash. And the nurse said it was as if Monsieur Treillet had wanted to kill himself.

Emerald then visited the site of the crash. The flimsy aircraft was still there, scattered on the rocks, a few bits of the fuselage wrapped round a tree trunk close to the water. One piece of fabric was flapping like a flag in the breeze. It seemed a miracle that the pop star had been pulled out alive.

When Emerald went on duty that evening she took over from another nurse in charge of the patient. She sensed after a while that Treillet might be able to hear her despite his coma.

She needed someone to talk to. Her own biopsy readings a week earlier had given her a huge shock. She began whispering to him that she had leukaemia. The infection of her blood was fast worsening and would become chronic, she was told. No doubt she could hope for occasional respites, periods of stability, but the verdict was grim. She had six months to a year to live. Emerald kept this appalling news to herself, not wishing to cause anguish to her parents or her boyfriend, the junior doctor. Meanwhile she was understandably pent up and was glad to pour out her hopes and fears to Treillet as he lay in her care in a coma. It was her impression that he was fighting back quite well, as Dr. Koln had said. And if Treillet could fight, so could she.

Bob's face, calm and expressionless, remained before her whenever she returned to her cramped twelfth floor, two room flatlet. She had chosen the top floor of the tower block because it gave her a sense of freedom, as if she were a little bird who could fly away and come back at will. This place was her first stop to liberty, she told herself when she moved in. At that time she had plans to join the Médecins Sans Frontières team in Cambodia, but her parents had implored her to stay in France, and her colleagues scoffed at her plans, seeing them as a passing fancy. And now that she had leukaemia she would never fly away.

Treillet continued watching her on the computer screen until the first ray of sunlight entered the hospital room. She looked stunning in her contour-hugging tunic as she began collecting her things to go off duty. For an instant, he felt pretty much like a voyeur in a celestial sex shop, an idea that made him want to giggle. But, wow, she was an attractive, desirable woman. When he'd first seen her on the screen at the Centre, he at once recognized her for the kind of girl he'd always dreamed of but never seemed to meet. All the others faded from his imagination when he saw her.

Without warning the junior doctor slunk into the room with a finger to his lips. Bob's mood changed instantly to one of fierce jealousy. The guy stalked over and inched her back to the wall, unbuttoning her tunic, then he played with her breasts, smothering her with smoochy kisses. Treillet deduced that they were going steady as a couple. Emerald tried to push him away but he refused to accept her resistance. Struggling, she looked almost as if she were begging the singer to come to her help. Yet, curiously, her eyes were on his own comatose form.

To his amazement the earthly Treillet actually smiled! It was not much of a smile, but it was undeniably a response to her gaze. How could this be? It dawned on him of a sudden that the smile came from his Other Self. The rotten sod meant to have it off with her, while he himself was absent and powerless to foil him. Of all the lousy tricks!

All this time, the sand in Archie Mackenzie's egg timer had been falling slowly but relentlessly.

Bob knew he had to make a decision – to stay or go back to Earth. Only a few grains of sand were left. On the one hand he had no wish to join up with his Other Self in his debilitated body. On the other hand the prospect of waiting at the U.S.C. for his Other Self to turn up did not bear thinking about.

It occurred to him that, if he believed in the Love-Serenity-Faith formula with all his might, the code would logically be compatible with his superb scheme for a Union for Renovating the Planet. Certainly the U.R.P. clashed with the pacifist policy that held sway up here, so it was no good staying. Back on Earth, the U.R.P. would need to fight to save mankind; bloodless revolutions had very occasionally taken place in a limited area, but never worldwide.

He recalled the affair of the tramps. He had let a couple of hobos sleep in his garage, admittedly against the advice of his Other Self. And in a matter of days the garage was occupied by a dozen or so more layabouts. Then one weekend while he was doing a show in Nice, the garage went up in flames following a fist fight among the visitors. On returning home he discovered that they had broken into the cottage itself before clearing off, stolen his best wine and relieved him of some valuable trinkets and his ready cash. Evidently they believed that charity began at home, someone else's home.

For weeks after the incident he refused to give a donation to any cause whatsoever, least of all to street people. From now on, the only cause he would be interested in was himself. Later his collective ideology took hold of him once more, his vision returned of a brave new world living in harmony, though modified by his Other Self who assured him he was wasting his time. Two millenniums after the crucifixion, the Other Self pointed out, human beings were still at one another's throats, so what would Bob Treillet, simple mortal, hope to achieve with his fancy brainwave? Mankind was a lost cause, you could do precious little for the great mass of people whose idea of perfection was stuffing themselves with a pizza while watching some fatuous TV quiz game. No wonder the Almighty had thrown the towel in.

Treillet realized as he glared at the egg timer that he was in a double bind. Not only was he caught between two worlds, he also had no clear idea what to do about it, and he even doubted whether he should do anything at all. If the Supreme Power had given up, he himself as a mere human was unlikely to change mankind. He hung on to the idea through pride, his Other Self would doubtless tell him, whereas he believed he really had a mission that had a pure motive. Bob felt like a condemned man waiting for the guillotine blade to fall.

He remembered another incident in his tumultuous existence, the Bastille Day revolution at Saint-Tropez. He had a notion that, since Saint-Tropez was one of the key centres of the planet media-wise, it might be the ideal spot for a sensational statement of protest. The stinking rich from the four corners of the world had their yachts tied up in the harbour, in full view of the stream of sightseers shuffling past green with envy. There could hardly be a better backdrop for a commando operation, a grandiose anarchist happening, a firework display to beat all firework displays.

Around 4 a.m. on that July 14, Bob drove to the old harbour in a water company repair van stolen the previous evening. He wore a Robespierre style wig to conceal his identity, judging that he would be mistaken for a late reveller returning to his yacht. He parked the van and walked onto a pier where five enormous vessels were tied up side by side. Nobody noticed the plastic bag he was carrying with his Molotov cocktails.

His purpose was not to maim or kill, but simply to draw attention to the insolent wealth of the influential few alongside the disgraceful poverty of the working (and non-working) masses loaded down with debt and taxes and suchlike. Unseen, he launched his attack and scampered back to the van as several horrendous blasts rocked the town. Minutes later the dockside was cluttered with lady refugees in mink duffel coats hugging their Gucci bags of diamonds, gazing wistfully as their menfolk in silk pyjamas fought to stop their tax-haven investments disappearing in smoke. Two vessels sank forthwith and the stench of burning teak and leather lay heavy on the resort for several weeks. An emir anchored offshore staged a giant couscous and champagne breakfast to mark the event.

The local authorities were less delighted. The restaurant and hotel and fashion store proprietors stormed the city hall demanding action. A Senegalese statuette vendor was almost lynched. Gendarmes from a wide radius were rushed to the scene and were told they would have to forego their siesta.

The media kept the story on the front pages for days, and the flow of sightseers quadrupled in the weeks that followed. Then everything returned to normal.

Bob had a close shave. Owing to his past record, he was taken in for questioning. He had his alibi ready; he claimed he had spent the night with a lady friend at his cottage and the partner in question confirmed that they had breakfast in bed. No, she hadn't heard a thing around 4 a.m., she always wore earplugs in bed.

Thus when the final grain of sand passed through the gullet of the egg timer, Treillet still wasn't sure that he wanted to save the human race at all. His powers of judgement had forsaken him, his emotions were at zero, his mind a blank.

It was then that he noticed on the computer screen that the instrument next to the Eurasian nurse depicting his brain activity was showing a flat line. As the sound blips changed to a single note, the girl grabbed a phone and gabbled something into it. Clearly distraught, she clenched her hands together like some heroine in a silent film, apparently urging her patient to keep on fighting for his life.

Presently heavy footsteps approached, the door burst open and Dr. Koln marched into the room. He instructed the nurse to leave him alone with the patient, telling her that to all intents and purposes the pop star had pooped out.

The Chief Surgeon took a mighty gulp of air and prepared for action.

Koln was acquainted with death, his ultimate foe, his sparring partner night and day. Since the loss of his wife, and later of his son, he had scarcely had a proper night's sleep. The boy had died in a motorbike accident shortly after telling Koln that he was HIV positive and ultimately would probably get AIDS. His father wondered if the crash were really an accident, and regretted not being closer to his son when he was alive. As a result his nights were marred with self-recrimination and fearful dreams in which death took on physical shape, mocking him as he tried to comfort his wife and son. In one repetitive nightmare his wife's face poked out from a black cloud as she watched the lad moaning and wrestling with human entrails. Koln would wake, sweating profusely, his face bathed in tears. Sometimes the surgeon, eminent though he was, wondered whether he was going mad.

He stood by his patient Treillet, brandishing a syringe like a Kalashnikov gun, assessing what and where to inject. Treillet's brain may or may not have fallen victim to death's onslaught but he could still help him fight a final battle by stimulating the heart, the lungs, the liver or the remaining kidney. Koln glanced again at the heartbeat screen, judging that a cardiac arrest was a probability. He quickly filled the syringe and, using a cardiac regulator, plunged the needle into Bob's nearest forearm. Then he observed the patient, moving from one side of the bed to the other.

There was no evident change and Koln shut his eyes tight. Watching the screen, Bob supposed that he was praying silently, disappointed by the limits of medical science, Koln might even be reciting a black mass of some kind. And then Bob noticed that a vague shape was forming perhaps fifty centimetres above the bed. Gradually the shape stabilized and became more compact. The surgeon saw it too and his jaw dropped. After perhaps a minute the shape assumed the dimensions of a human being, a man closely similar to Treillet himself. Moreover the shape was now attached via a sort of umbilical cord to the back of the patient's head where the bump came at the base of the cranium.

To his dismay, Treillet realized that this shape was his Other Self leaving his body, implying that actual death was imminent! Indeed, the brain and the heart screens were now flat, both emitting steady notes.

Koln shot his arms in the air and released a stream of curses in his mother tongue. Placing a pair of electrodes to the chest, he switched on a defibrillator as determinedly as Wagner's Parsifal going after the Holy Grail.

Bob's body shook in spasms, but the two instruments still emitted continuous tones. Meanwhile the cloud in the air slowly rose, finally disappearing through the ceiling. No need to ask for whom the bell tolls, Treillet whispered to himself. He wondered why Koln was persisting with the electrodes. Couldn't he see that the end had come? As P.G. Wodehouse had put it, Treillet had handed in his dinner pail.

Bob was wrong. Koln kept going with the electric shock treatment and eventually a blip appeared on the heart screen, and then a few more, accompanied shortly by renewed blips on the brain screen.

'He's done it, he's done it!' Treillet shouted. 'Good old King Koln! Deutschland Uber Alles! Vive l'Europe! I am still alive, but the Other Self has skedaddled.'

He longed to be in the room with Koln, congratulating him. Whether the surgeon would have noticed him was open to doubt, for he was busily checking over the patient, frowning and muttering to himself for all the world like a plumber trying to remove an air lock. He had obviously dismissed the mysterious cloud as a hallucination, preferring to get on with the task in hand. Koln was not a man to entertain such nebulous ideas as spirits, auras, souls, alter egos and spooks. Koln was a man of science.

As for Treillet, if his Other Self had really scampered, he was at liberty to go ahead with the U.R.P. project unhampered. Yessir, the wheel of chance had come up with his lucky number. Fortune had favoured the brave in preference to the cowardly Other Self.

Love-Serenity-Faith was all set to transform the world. There was no time to lose, he must get back to Earth.

* * *

After much thinking, Daisy had resolved to accept her state of being dead and was starting her mea culpa in order to expiate her earthly faults. Strangely enough, her hatred towards Archie was gradually fading away. Her sudden leniency towards her colleague did not extend to Zior whom she would never forgive for undermining her hopes. It wasn't worth living her life in respect for a high moral and religious cult if it produced such a pitiful end result. No doubt about it, the divine authority made a mistake with her. Error or not, it was dreadfully unfair rejecting her as a vulgar sinner. Such ungratefulness was incomprehensible to her as well as unacceptable. Before the Supreme Power struck her down, Daisy meant to do everything that her principles forbade her when she was alive.

Since both she and Archie were suspended from duty, they must make common cause against their employer. After all, Archibald wasn't an ill-disposed fellow in himself, she felt. Probably he was right, she was as much to blame as he was for their constant squabbling. It took two to make an argument, and arguing could become a habit if you weren't careful. She glanced somewhat fondly at him as he stood forlornly on the steps of the office.

There was this to be said in favour of losing your job – you were a free agent. Freedom was a concept virtually unknown to Daisy, whose life had been dominated by what you had to do rather than what you wanted to do. A woman in her position at the palace had no business even thinking about freedom; you obeyed the call of duty, you adhered to tradition, you forced events to comply with pre-set plans, you got on with your job. As a result she had never had any fun out of life worth mentioning. Her devotion to the crown and the Christian ethic had been sincere, and now that it had all turned sour, she had nothing to show for her assiduous loyalty.

A wave of feminist revolt uplifted her. If she were a free agent, there was no reason why she should continue to be cowed and frightened. Not for nothing had the women's liberation movement made such progress in recent times.

Surely, she had as much right to emancipation as her sisters.

Taking the argument a step further, she began to suspect that the very rules and principles that had held her in thrall might be open to debate. They might even be a lot of poppycock. Sin, for example, seemed to be very much a personal matter, the transgressions of yesterday being today's accepted behaviour. What huge changes had occurred in that sphere in the past half century!

Daisy began mulling over the seven capital sins – pride, envy, anger, sloth, avarice, gluttony and lust.

Pride was simply a nuisance that had served only to make her relations with Archie a misery. Envy was never a real problem for her, whose royal employers suffered as much from their place in life as everyone else. Besides, in Daisy's present state, eyeing the place of the Queen wouldn't make sense any more; on the other hand, she wouldn't mind Zior's job. Her anger took the form of justified indignation over the treatment she and Archie had received on arrival at the Centre, notably in the immediate past. Sloth was certainly not her problem, so she could dismiss that. Avarice had amounted solely to defending her territory in the office, and the office no longer existed as part of her life.

As to gluttony, she had to admit that it possessed an element of appeal. To be honest she would have loved at that moment to gorge herself with some of those goodies she had never dared to touch, except in her weaker lapses: fat nutty oysters and champagne just like Churchill used to stuff himself with, a mixed grill in the good old British tradition complete with kidneys and mushrooms and Worcester Sauce, alternatively a coq au vin accompanied by a really good burgundy, toasted teacakes with lashings of butter, luscious creamy cakes made with her favourite liqueur (Benedictine of course), exciting chocolates from Fortnum and Mason … Daisy's mouth watered at the thought, she could almost taste the victuals gratifying her taste buds as they slipped over her tongue.

Last but not least there was lust. She recalled a phrase from a rather naughty article in a women's magazine she picked up in the dentist's waiting room. 'Orgasm – the most wonderful experience known to Woman ...' At the time she had passed it over, unsure what it meant, assuming it was something to do with the funny feeling that came over her as she drank her Ovaltine in bed last thing at night. It was a nice enough sensation but it made her go hot between the sheets, which was annoying. It seemed now as she looked back on those moments that she must have missed out on the alleged greatest experience. Well, she jolly well wouldn't miss out on it any more if she got half the chance, or her name was not Lady Daisy Sniffington-Madley.

Archie was still standing on the office steps, and she sidled over to him.

'Archibald – Archie, my pet,' she said. 'Since you are so knowledgeable on the subject, I think we ought to have a little chat about sex.'

Mackenzie went rigid, his mouth opened to the size of a small orange and he whipped his hands over his crotch.

'What!!!' he yelped. 'I mean, sure Daisy. What you wanna know? There's a lot to it.'

Her ladyship placed a foot on the lowermost step and a hand on her hip. She pulled her skirt up over her knee, fiddled with her hair and laughed gaily.

'Archie dear, don't be startled. You look like a goose that's discovered what paté foie gras is made from. Ever since I've known you, you've been telling me tales of your romps in the hay. I'd like to try it. In fact, I insist on trying it.'

'Miracles never cease,' he gulped. 'What's come over you? Have you eaten something nasty?'

'You never said it was nasty, making love I mean. I've always been well-behaved and my bedside reading has been limited to books on etiquette and domestic science. I didn't even dare read *Gone With the Wind.* Anyway, I've never enjoyed myself as other people do and it's high time I made up for that. Everyone does it, or at least they ought to if the experience is as lovely as they say.'

She slipped an arm into his and began walking him round the grounds.

'My intention upon retirement was to sell my place in Sussex and go out and join the Mother Teresa Foundation in India. I saw that as my final sacrifice on behalf of the Almighty. But the Almighty decided otherwise. I was posted here prematurely, only to be treated as if I'd spent my earthly life in a bawdy house instead of a palace. I consider myself cheated.'

'You mean you wanted to go down in history books as some kind of a saint, saving sinners and scraping up the corpses from the Calcutta sidewalks.'

'Something of the sort,' she said proudly. 'I wanted to be useful, but I landed up here and Zior had the cheek to ask me what I had done with my life. It's now obvious to me that I made life frightfully shabby for the staff I had under me. I gladly admit it now.'

'Instead of sinners, you saved the Queen, but damned the sinners?'

'Exactly, and they probably damned me. Anyhow I suppose I have got my just deserts. However, it looks like being quite boring here from now on with nothing to do. We need an interest, and I thought of sex.'

'Oh you did, did you?'

'I really can't understand why the authorities up here are so beastly. What have we done that's so terrible? And especially what have I done?'

'Nothing much, by the sound of it. I guess you believed in damnation.'

'Of course, it's mentioned in the Bible, lots of times in fact.'

'You don't read the right parts of it. Get this straight, the Divine Light wants us all in Heaven, as I understand it, so it has to be very catholic in its beliefs.'

'Catholic!' Daisy spluttered. 'Good grief, I'm still Church of England, you realize. I am no scarlet woman!'

'OK, OK. Keep your knickers on. Even so, teaching you sex is like asking Zior to do the rumba.'

'I don't care. Before it's too late, I mean to have the great experience. I've a right to sex like everyone else. I want the whole shooting match.'

'Yeah, well, you gotta lead up to it, as you might say. Do you figure Treillet will go along with this?'

'Treillet? Who's talking about Treillet? Look, Archie, you're a man and I'm a woman. So let's just do it.'

She gave Mackenzie a peck on the cheek and skipped round to face him.

'Come on darling, make an effort, I'm sure you like me a teeny-weeny bit. We can get something going.'

'It's a tough assignment and this plastic body of mine ain't gonna make it any easier.'

'You know the technique, you'll work something out. All you need is a little enthusiasm, get the old brain cells clicking, use your imagination. We can improvise as we go along. We're wasting time so hold me tight and give me a big hug and a kiss to start with.'

Archie doffed his bowler and obeyed. Suddenly Daisy rushed off behind some bushes.

'Hey, not so fast,' he protested.

'I'm only changing into my other clothes. Zior gave us two different outfits to choose, remember. My other one is hidden here.'

Her head popped up from the bushes. 'Archie, I've just discovered something spiritually astonishing,' she said with a light of ecstasy on her face, looking as devoted as Saint Elizabeth herself. 'I realize now that death is too grim and complicated a subject to take seriously, and all that agonizing stuff about redemption is too confusing for words.'

'OK, if you say so.'

'Don't run out on me,' Daisy cooed. 'I'll be ready in a jiffy.' She gave a peal of wanton glee.

Treillet was doing exercises. He lay on his back with his arms along his sides, breathing slowly and deeply.

His idea was to limber up for transcendental meditation so as to clear his mind of all negative thinking.

While breathing he spoke the code letters L-S-F, simultaneously picturing symbols corresponding to the three letters. Love presented itself as a mother hugging a skunk in her arms. Serenity was a patriarchal type of man contemplating a nuclear blast on the horizon while smoking a pipe in the comfort of a deckchair. Faith's mental picture consisted of a Norwegian, a Red Indian, a North Korean and an Australian aborigine holding hands looking at a newspaper headline reading 'Wall Street Debacle'. He concentrated hard so that the three images became anchored in his mind, chasing away all tension and anger.

It was plain to Bob that, if he could join up again with his earthly body, practising the composure of the Dalai Lama, his Other Self would find him unassailable. No doubt this was asking a lot of his flesh and blood, but if the flesh were weak his spirit would be strong and he would triumph over the shortcomings of medical science.

From behind the bushes, Daisy emerged wearing a leopard-skin jacket, a shiny green low necked blouse, a red miniskirt with a side slit, fishnet stockings and high heels. Her hair in its severe bun was now concealed in a splendid curly blond wig. She had cheeks that glowed with pink make-up, her mouth shone with crimson lipstick and her false nails sparkled with crack-proof varnish. Her eye shadow was black with desire.

'Now I've seen everything,' Archie rasped as she advanced upon him.

'Not yet, sweetie,' she quipped, swaying her hips and dangling a black handbag from an arm. 'How's this for starters? Claudia Schiffer never looked like this, I'm the queen of the catwalk.'

'I've seen better queens in Los Angeles, but we'll let that pass. All that's missing is a whip.'

He cut the air with his cane. Daisy pouted at him. 'You think it is a bit overdone?'

'Hell no. Death would be pretty grim without a bit of hanky-panky.'

'You're just playing hard to get. I have a little present for you, I know you'll love it.'

She crossed one knee over the other and giggled like a schoolkid showing her tits behind the bike sheds.

Her self-styled majesty drew a tiny package from her handbag and told him to open it. He undid the string and tore the paper open, to find a pair of red and green panties with black lace edging.

'Really Daisy, you are too kind. Let me tell you something. If I could have brought just one thing with me up here, only one thing, I would have brought my collection of ladies panties. Cabinets stuffed with such cute ones. With them I could have enjoyed my fetish through eternity. And you my dear, honestly, what would you have brought along with you?'

'The Order of the Royal Tablecloth. The day Her Majesty decorated me with that was the greatest thrill I've had so far, I don't think anything could ever equal the extreme pleasure. Unless, of course, you can prove otherwise.'

Archie stroked his face with the red and green panties.

'I knew you'd like them, I know your style. They are still warm, you'll notice.'

'You mean …'

'Exactly. I've nothing more to lose but my honour.'

She burst into a cascade of joyous laughter.

'I'm so excited, this is going to be a wonderful first time ever. Oh, Archie, I want you, I need you. Show me everything you've ever done to a woman. I want to know it all, from the very romantic caress up to the kinkiest discovery.'

Mackenzie lifted her off the ground, and headed for a group of rhododendrons.

'With these plastic bodies of ours,' he said, 'this ought to be quite fascinating.'

5

The American senator John Warden was on the computer screen helping some handicapped children into a bus for a revival of *Annie* on Broadway. The bus got stuck in a traffic jam, then it drove on at a snail's pace and Bob caught sight of a billboard for *Manhattan Follies*. The illustration was of a tap dancer with a cane and a bowler hat, and the message said the show was choreographed by a certain Paul Zbigeskwirtski, assisted by Archie Mackenzie.

Treillet blinked in astonishment. Archie had told him that it was he who had worked up the entire choreography of the show. Either he'd been telling lies again, or this Zbigeskwirstki guy had pushed Archie into second place after he'd turned up his toes. That was highly interesting, he might be able to use that information to his own advantage some time in the future.

Seeing the billboard reminded him of his Other Self. It wouldn't be a bad idea if they could end their war of attrition, uniting as one. Next time he had the Eurasian nurse on the screen he would suggest she have a little talk with his life-long adversary. The only snag was how to contact her. If all else failed he might try going through a medium.

In a flash of inspiration he thought of Honorine, Olga's sidekick, the tubby girl who wanted to form a fan club for him. Nice girl, Honorine, she possessed occult powers. Yes, he must get through to Honorine.

Archie and Daisy rose from their lovemaking in the rhododendrons. Daisy slowly buttoned her blouse and zipped up her diminutive skirt. She had an expression of total fulfilment on her visage.

'Well Archie,' she gurgled, 'I must say I'm enormously grateful to you. What a stallion you turned out to be! I never imagined it would be so good. Tell me, in what category would you rate me? Vaginal or clitoridienne, as the French would put it; considering the peculiar situation we're in up here, I imagine it's difficult to answer.'

'Daisy, my sweet, you are in a category of your own. If you didn't exist you'd have to be invented.'

'How fortunate that it's all in the mind,' she proclaimed as if sex had become her field of expertise. 'I was dreading actual penetration. Oh those delicious naughty words, they did bring me on so! I shall live it all over again and again as long as I live – I mean, as long as I'm here. I loved the preliminaries, your heavenly erotic images, with no hint of vulgarity. I thrilled to your caresses, to your smooth gestures when you undressed me. You made me feel so beautiful, a princess surrendering to her prince charming. Utterly romantic. And then you gave me my very first orgasm, thank you awfully for finding my G-spot. Isn't that what you called it? Oh lord how innocent I was before, I thought the G-spot had something to do with the gear lever on my Range Rover. Archie, we'll do it often, won't we?'

'You put me in a spot, honey,' Archie mumbled, and in an aside: 'Women are all the same, give 'em an inch and they'll take a mile.'

'Archie, I have a secret I wish to reveal,' she declared, scanning the grounds with the haughty look of a cardinal at a conclave.

'Go on.'

'I must tell you what happened after that awful business with the duke, my grandfather. I never even mentioned it to the palace chaplain, such a good soul, he was the Rev. Plantagenet-Balderdash. Well after that terrible experience, there was no question of intimacy with a man. I was so upset it was agony simply shaking hands with men and I fondly imagined that I would never know love, that wedded bliss would never come my way. Besides, with all the semen they were putting into deep freeze, women didn't need men any more. Apart from which I would have had an abortion if I were expecting a boy.'

'That's a foetus who will never know how lucky he was to avoid you as a mother.'

'Nobody is perfect,' she said. 'Anyway, soon after I entered the royal household I took a liking to one of the ladies-in-waiting.'

'Daughter of Lord Buckethead?'

'Certainly not. She was a distant cousin of some Bulgarian prince whose name I could never pronounce. We knew her as Ursula and she took me into her confidence, she worshipped me. And one night during a violent storm, she asked me to share her four-poster bed as she was frightened. But of course we did nothing wrong. She wasn't a lesbian.'

'Whew,' said Archie, wiping his brow. 'Nothing happened that time anyway.'

'Nothing ever did,' Daisy expostulated. 'The very idea, messing about with another woman! Imagine the headlines: Palace Dykes in Romps Row Drama; Four-poster Parties Banned – Premier Resigns. The nation would never have got over it. However, as time went by, it was I who had lecherous designs on her, I became hopelessly infatuated with her.'

'So you became head over heels in love with her.'

'I could do nothing about it. Except for one thing, I carried out a small operation on myself.'

'An operation. . .'

'Yes, a clitoridectomy.'

'Holy shit, you didn't!' cried Archie.

'I jolly well did, borrowed a knife from the kitchen. But there's no need to go into details.'

The knife was the beginning of her grim devotion to duty. Her grandfather had stolen her innocence, Ursula had spoilt her love life and the palace staff had paid the consequences.

Now it was too late to look back. Daisy had no choice but to go forward. She had to chase out of her guilty mind all those bad thoughts and everlasting regrets and look ahead with prudent optimism to an uncertain future.

Hitching up her skirt and adjusting a stocking top, Daisy went on: 'Now perhaps you realize how much I need you, darling. Love me please, I've fallen for you, I want to get laid over and over again, I want to marry you.'

'I'll have to think about it,' Archie muttered.

'Well hurry up about it.'

'That's the problem, it needs a lot of reflection. Not so long ago you were chewing my nuts off, every chance you got. We'd have to be sure this'll turn out for the better, we could be putting our heads in a noose.'

'Amor vincit omnia, Archie dear.'

'I told that once to a girl in Greenwich Village. She said she'd have the chilli con carne instead.'

Daisy strolled around with him some more. 'You know, our voyager in transit is rather nice in his own peculiar way.'

'You're walking out on me already?'

'Haven't you read those Masters and Johnson books? All modern women have adventures outside marriage. Treillet would be my chilli con carne.'

'You're a real glutton, almost debauched.'

'Debauched! You sound like the Pope all of a sudden. Since when has lovemaking been something to do with debauchery? As far as I am concerned, we've made love, haven't we? You can't compare that beautiful act of purity with a misdemeanour that I would like to have with Treillet. You mustn't be shocked, Archie. Love is one thing, a tiny adventure now and again is another. You have opened my vistas.'

They walked in silence from then on. Mackenzie was glad to have co-operated with her. Even so, his sole motive had been to calm her down by responding to her need. It seemed that he had merely succeeded in putting a match to her volcano, and there was no stopping her now that she had tasted forbidden fruit. Disaster lay ahead, he was sure. The ways of the Lord may be impenetrable to the human mind, but the divinity was unlikely to change the rules just for Daisy; if it were wrong to bed-hop when you were alive, it must be just as wrong when you were dead.

The letters R.I.P. – Rest in Peace – were a wish and a promise for those who quit their life on earth. At that moment, they seemed more like a rip-off. You couldn't play fast and loose with the Supreme Power's do's and don'ts.

He gave a quick sideways glance at his companion. Her eyes bulged, her tongue lolled out on one side of her face, her cheeks were flushed. Hers was the face of lust, she was concupiscence in person, and a deep melancholy came over him.

'You'll never get away with it,' was all he said.

Loud and clear, Honorine got the telepathic message from Bob, and she hastened to the hospital.

She was experienced in the paranormal, regularly picking up the wavelengths of lost souls the world over.

In accordance with the general practice in these matters, when the S.O.S. arrived, she placed a voodoo object at each corner of Treillet's bed: a tuft of hair, a hen's leg, crushed bone powder, a wooden figurine.

Olga Paslov looked on, a sneer of contempt on her face; her own reaction to Bob's message would have been to put out a press statement and release the song Death to My Other Half.

Honorine had consulted her first cousin's uncle's ninth wife's granddad to check on the most effective procedure in the case of apparent clinical death. And she now gently placed her hands over Bob's face to transmit the old marabout's powers. Honorine had prepared a pad and ballpoint and, as she went into her trance, her hand responded to the automatic writing conveyed back to her.

Olga, who only half believed in such jiggery-pokery, stood behind the fat girl trying to figure out the spidery words as they went down on the pad. When it was over and Honorine was herself again, Olga saw that Honorine's face was awash with tears. Her features were contorted in horror and her complexion turned a whiter shade of brown.

On the pad was a stark and simple message: 'I want to die, I want to die.'

The door was flung open and Dr Koln entered. Honorine jumped and tried to hide the pad in her bag. Koln took one look at the voodoo things on the bed, and held out his hand for the pad.

Koln scowled at it and barked: 'Nein, nein, nein. Er ist nicht kaput!'

His eyes rivetted on the computer screen at the Centre, Bob flung his arms up: 'Oh, no, that's not what I want, I didn't send that. Some idiot has garbled it!'

He concentrated and sent another message: 'I want to live, repeat live. Contact Other Self now. Will unite to vanquish death. Acknowledge, play back and expedite – Treillet.'

Bob wasn't too pleased with 'expedite' but it was too late to mess around with the thing any more. His Other Self had put gremlins in the dispatch.

While Bob was composing the second message, Koln was tearing into the two girls. He was mad with rage, his ranting confused.

'Abortion already a bad thing is,' he bellowed. 'Euthanasia against oath. Never oh never. I not murder will commit! Hypocrates ja, hypocrisy nicht gut! You, charlatan witch, the hospital must leave. Olga keep mouth shut, I see you later. Koln pro-life!'

A loud sigh of relief escaped Treillet, up above. Whatever happened, Koln was on his side.

Daisy drifted through the wall into the room, strode over to the computer and switched it off. She wore her old clothes and began prowling around him in a wide circle like a lioness seeking to devour him.

'Hello Bobby,' she said in a sultry voice. 'We're on our own, just the two of us. That's nice. Let's not beat about the bush. I want you, sweetie pie, and I mean to have you.'

Treillet tried to push her off as she sprang at him. 'Help, murder, rape!!! Get off me, you crazy old crone.'

She tore off his tunic.

'It's too late to pray now, silly boy. The Supreme Power is not interested, he's abandoned us all, including you. We are all damned, it's apocalypse now, the Valkyries are here, you can't escape me!'

Daisy had him on the floor now and was flinging off her skirt, to display a pair of long peach coloured drawers dotted with sequins.

Bob was shrieking for help, calling on Archie.

Daisy did a wild belly dance, obscenely rolling her haunches and shaking her withered boobs. She squealed with delight as blasts from a Wagnerian overture rent the air. She rubbed a make believe microphone against her pubis, yowling out the melody of the orchestra.

In other circumstances, this amazing libertine act would have amused Bob. He couldn't believe his own eyes. Daisy was actually committing blasphemy.

Mackenzie suddenly appeared, and began jumping and roaring with huge gusts of laughter. He clapped to the music's rhythm, encouraging her to live out her act of profanity. She had to exorcise the demons hidden away deep in her soul desperately searching for repentance.

Daisy hooted, flinging off her bloomers. She came to a halt. The music changed to the regular whump-whump of an old Rolling Stones' song: Sympathy for the Devil. She stood facing Treillet with her legs apart, knees bent, jerking her middle back and forth to the beat again and again in a primitive portrayal of copulation. On and on she went and a greedy smirk appeared on her hungry mouth. Her lips were swollen, her mousy hair awry, her eyes like saucers.

Now she went rigid and held her breath, her face screwed up and she doubled over in a Neanderthal orgasm, sinking to the floor where she writhed out the last ounces of her pleasure, whimpering with joy.

The music faded away. Perhaps ten silent seconds went by, and Bob ventured a giggle. Mackenzie leaned against a wall, observing her ladyship's crumpled form.

'Sow the wind and you reap a hurricane,' he said quietly.

Daisy lifted her head. 'I had to have it. I've got my revenge on Satan. He pestered me all my life, and now I've called his bluff. I have eaten the fruit of the knowledge of Evil.'

Uncurling, she rose awkwardly to her feet. She walked slowly towards him with a suspicious look on her face. All of a sudden, Archie seemed to her the Devil in person.

'Archie. It is you, isn't it Archie? B-but I can't believe it, you have altered, you are – Beelzebub. You are Satan. You've turned into Satan. You are the demon who gave the L-S-F code to that poor Treillet, who seduced me in the shrubbery, who is smiling craftily at me at this very instant!'

Mackenzie put his hand to his temples and waggled his forefingers skyward. He quipped: 'Have it your way, milady. OK I'm the Devil. Don't I look cute? Nonetheless, I ought to point out that this Beelzebub of yours might easily be a flight of the imagination, the mirror of your own lust. Your Beelzebub might in fact be Beelze-Bob! Funny thing, religion; if you believe in Heaven you have to believe in Hell, if you know God you gotta know Evil, if Virtue then Sin.'

Daisy's face hung as long as a dishcloth. She scrabbled around for her clothing, then turned again to Mackenzie.

'But one can't believe in nothing, nothing doesn't exist,' she moaned, her throat constricted. 'Oh dear, I don't know what I'm saying, I'm so confused.'

'Say nothing, sweetheart, it'll make a change.'

Daisy tucked her clothes under her arm, heading for the far wall, utterly miserable. Tears of despair streamed down her gaunt cheeks, the stigma of her profanity. She was the abomination of desolation, hunched over in the search for oblivion, for nothingness.

In the intensive care unit the clock showed 22.01. Bob could see Olga and Honorine creeping to the bed. It was hard to follow exactly what they were up to, as the sole illumination came from the corridor through the partition.

On tiptoe the girls felt their way, each with her lips pressed tightly together, Olga flashing a torch.

'All right,' Olga whispered. 'Let's run over it again. You take the torch and stand there. Don't move or you'll knock something over. I'll go round here and you shine the torch on my hands. When I've disconnected the oxygen, we both keep quiet with the torch out until I say "now" and then you shine the torch again so I can reconnect the tube. Then we clear out. I only hope you got Bob's message right.'

Honorine nodded. In view of the message 'I want to die, I want to die' that the pop star sent her, she imagined that he had chosen her to execute his last wish. The two women didn't suspect the existence of an Other Self. They had no way of guessing that Bob wanted to stay alive as much as his Other Self would rather he die.

In the white-walled room between life and death, Treillet was panic-stricken, calling out for Archie and Daisy. His Other Self must have intervened again to garble his second message designed to correct the first. Then he remembered that Koln had shooed the girls out just after the first message, which meant that Honorine's telepathic talent had been switched off at the crucial moment.

Honorine, invisible to Bob in the dark owing to her skin colour, was bewildered at his instruction, but was prepared to co-operate in carrying out his final wish. She had already decided to embark on a forty-day hunger strike at his grave-side to bring down her weight from 100 to sixty kilos. This would be her gift to the former pop star. At the same time she recalled that Jesus had risen from the dead after forty days and nights, and she had an idea He might perform a miracle for Bob and bring him back to life.

Olga, equally nonplussed at Bob's message, intended simply to help him on his way. If he wanted to pass away in dignity rather than suffer disablement for years on end, that was his right. A right that the medical world had refused to her father when he was dying of lung cancer. Olga had witnessed, powerless, the damage that the illness had done to the dignity of her dad. If one day another person dear to her had to go through such a suffering, she had vowed to carry out that person's wish.

Alerted by Treillet's cries, Archie and Daisy surged into the computer room.

'Where's that nurse, the chink, the Eurasian,' Archie snapped.

'I don't know,' said Bob. 'Haven't seen her all evening, she must be in a ward elsewhere, might be anywhere.'

'Send her a message at once,' Daisy ordered. 'While you're doing that, I'll handle the fatty.'

Just as Olga was about to disconnect the oxygen tube, Honorine fainted and the torch clattered to the floor next to the bed.

On the screen Treillet saw Emerald the Eurasian rushing along the corridor. She threw the door open.

'I had a presentiment that something was happening,' she panted. 'What are you doing here at this hour?'

'We called in to see how he is, we're returning to Paris,' said Olga, calm as a cucumber.

'What is she doing slumped over the chair like that?'

'She felt queer but she's all right.'

'Yes, I had a slight turn,' Honorine rejoined. 'I think we'll leave now, Olga, we don't want to interfere.'

When they were gone, the nurse checked the equipment and the patient, then left the room.

'That was a close shave,' Daisy said. 'With luck they won't try again.'

Archie watched the nurse clip-clopping along the corridor, and was surprised to feel a great tenderness towards her. She was a good girl, clearly devoted to her job. He was rather pleased that he was able to look upon a pretty woman without guessing the colour of her underwear. What's more, it occurred to him that she and Treillet would make a handsome couple.

'Nice girl, she'd suit you perfectly, Bob, keep you in order,' he said lightly.

'I hope it's not too late,' the singer muttered. 'Olga and Honorine might make another attempt to disconnect the lifeline.'

'What's the nurse's name?'

'Her badge says Emerald. Yes, she's a peach. If I shacked up with her, she'd maybe save me from my Other Self.'

'Who is this Other Self of yours?' Daisy asked urgently.

'A private matter,' Bob said.

Daisy never had much time for passive people who couldn't make up their minds. The very notion of split personality was abhorrent to her. Added to that she was extremely annoyed that Archibald had promised him the Earth, so to speak, when he revealed the L-S-F formula. Treillet was suspect, goodness knows what a volatile terrorist might do if he imagined he could become immortal and save the planet. What would the Almighty have to say if he started re-shaping Earth when he got back there? Of course, he and his so-called Other Self might end their quarrel, but an anarchist was always an anarchist. Treillet's precious Union for Renovating the Planet must be nipped in the bud. Such men were dangerous. Who would have thought that a thwarted corporal would one day bring about World War Two with the ridiculous notion of creating a race of supermen and an empire lasting 1,000 years? Bob Treillet might repeat the attempt, only worse. But how to stop him?

Archie's assessment of Bob was quite different. Like himself, he was an artist, and Mackenzie believed rightly or wrongly that artistic endeavour was the safest of all human activities. In the vast majority of cases, the artist was sincere and honest, as Treillet appeared to be. Naturally an artist at work often irritated the Establishment, but so did the Creator of the Universe, the greatest artist of all! Archie told himself that Mister Big Bang was on Treillet's side.

There was no doubt that Bob's vast project would force him to take a long shot at immortality. And, if his ideas disturbed the Establishment and made him, not the man of the year, but a man to be eliminated, the Church, faithful to her sense of opportunism, would jump at this chance to raise him to holy status. And in truth Archie deemed everyone would find something positive in the project and the Supreme Power would know how to recognize His own.

Daisy found it impossible to agree with this convoluted argument. She thought the whole sorry business should be reported to Zior. This was too big for them to handle. They simply could not let him loose down there to turn the place into some pseudo-Trotskyite rave-up. The fellow was a potential menace and if anything went wrong, they'd be left holding the baby. Besides, a matter of this importance was beyond the scope of such as the two of them, their wisdom was hardly better than Treillet's.

Archie said that the pop star deserved his chance and he begged Daisy to give him another twenty four hours. What was twenty four hours compared to eternity?

Flat on his back, arms by his sides, Treillet stared at the ceiling.

He realized that the moment had come to collect his senses, to gather together the loose fragments of his past and of his personality. In a word, to gain the plenitude he had been striving for ever since he stepped into the Universal Selection Centre after his accident. There was too much going on down there at the hospital to dilly-dally longer. He must take a cool hard look at himself.

Two entities cohabited to form Bob Treillet. He was two persons in one human. Here he was, a voyager with an astral body running round in circles, an egocentric, glib-speaking, demanding, near-hysterical, unappealing character in some ways with fancy ideas about himself and what he wanted to do. And then there was his secretive Other Self whom he had largely neglected during his active existence so far. If he could hope to make headway he had to come to terms with this melancholy partner, get to know him better, learn to co-exist with him. It was his only chance to gain confidence and lucidity.

His astral form slowly, almost imperceptibly, began rising from the floor, as he concentrated on the Love-Serenity-Faith formula.

Love now appeared to him as a full-bosomed woman giving the breast to a drug-addict gulping down the milk of human kindness.

Serenity was a boy scampering with a street gang inside a nuclear power station, the whole group of them becoming irradiated.

Faith was a gathering of people from the ends of the earth in a huge orgy of brotherhood.

At this juncture Treillet's train of thought was brutally interrupted by the clatter of a frenzied flamenco dance. He glanced round, saw Archie below him banging his feet in a cloud of dust – and promptly crashed to the floor.

'Aaaarrh,' he shouted, rolling over. 'You bungling fart, what the blazes are you up to?'

'Olé!' cried Archie. 'I've just found the way out for you.'

'I was getting close to it myself when you so rudely cut me off.'

'I can help you, provided my pest of a colleague doesn't make waves and the Supreme Power gives you a short period of grace.'

'And how long will that be?' Bob enquired, rising to his feet.

'Nobody can say, maybe five minutes, maybe longer. You've no time to lose, you have to act.'

'More thought and a little less clowning wouldn't do any harm,' Treillet threw back at him. 'I've had enough of your help already. A fat lot of good it's done me.'

Mackenzie extended his arms. 'Without a small supernatural shove on my part, you'll never sort yourself out. I'll give you your marching orders!'

Bob gave a sigh of exasperation. 'Well, let's have it. What's your brilliant idea this time?'

'As I understand the situation, you mean to use the L-S-F formula to help your fellow men. You're aiming at justice for all.'

'Affirmative.'

'The snag is there is only one kind of justice on Earth – death the great leveller. That being so, immortality solves nothing. There never will be a level playing field if immortality gets a look in.'

'That's one way of approaching the problem. But you have to agree that it will take an eternity to clear up the mess down there. Are people any happier than they were a hundred years ago? There's a labour of Hercules waiting for me.'

Archie flapped his hands at Treillet. 'Sure sure, but be reasonable. You won't get far with worn out slogans like "Make love not war".'

'I've thought of that. It might help just the same. What I basically want is to confirm once and for all that there is an after-life, that human beings can make a success of it if they look to their own destiny, take their lives into their own hands.'

Mackenzie shook his head. 'You're very naive. Face the facts, Bob. For every person who wants to do something, there are nine others wanting to do something else, and a great army of people who never do anything at all that you'd notice. And don't tell me it's the fault of The System. People like you have been trying to change The System for several millenniums, and it is still there. It's like democracy, you can shout and bawl what you like, but you can't do anything about The System.'

'So it's back to the jungle?' Bob asked. 'Democracy can be made to evolve for the better, but above all we'll never get anywhere without respecting the freedom of others.'

'Huh, will you yourself follow that ideal as a militant anarchist? You know what anarchy really means? No water, no gas, no trains, no buses, nothing to eat, garbage piled up on the sidewalks, corpses floating down the rivers. Is that what you want? Not much freedom about that.'

They were both silent for a long moment.

'Where's Daisy?' asked Treillet at length, for something to say.

'Dunno. I left her wandering in the grounds singing Land of Hope and Glory. She's as mixed up as you are.'

'See here Archie, I can only give you my word, I'm a new kind of anarchist, you'll see. What else do you want from me?'

'I want the person who's nearest your heart.'

'Emerald! What is this, some kind of extortion trick?'

'I may be a fool but I'm not stupid. She's yours if she'll have you. No Bob, I'll take you instead.'

'Me? Of all the half-witted things to say.'

'Let me put it this way. When you reach the stage of clinical death, you have your return ticket torn up for you. Your only option now is to persuade your Other Self to join you here.'

Bob was aghast. 'I – I can't go back?'

'You have crossed the frontier. Earth is a no-go area for you now.'

'A likely story. Tell me another one. I demand to see the Supreme Power. He'll listen to my ideas.'

'Zior has spoken, he makes no exceptions. So forget it. You will remain a voyager in transit until your Other Self is dead. As a schizo you're unique, we've never had one at the Centre until you dropped in. That ought to please you, you have always wanted to be different, someone special, like those Liverpool boys.'

Mackenzie raised his arms in a well-that's-it gesture, and turned to leave. Softly he hummed the Beatles' ditty:

'When I find myself in trouble
Mother Mary comes to me
Speaking words of wisdom
Let it be, let it be ...'

Bob took hold of Mackenzie's arm. 'By the way, talking of show business, do you know a man by the name of Zbigeskwirtski?'

Archie spun round, his ears stuck up like a dobermann hearing the tinkle of a broken window pane.

'Sure I do,' he rasped guardedly. 'He was my assistant on the *Manhattan Follies* show. He'll go far.'

'Well he's top of the bill already. Choreographer of the show.'

'What! Who told you that?'

'Nobody. I saw it on the computer system.'

'The hell you did. You mean you found out how to work it?'

'I found a software virus, I guess. What's the Supreme Power going to think of that? You were supposed to be the genius behind the show. He'll be disappointed to say the least. Look Archie, I'm prepared to do a deal with you. I will let you have the secret of the virus, if I receive my freedom. How's that for fair play? Think about it, for five minutes let's say. It could be your last five minutes before you meet your Maker.'

Bob waved him away, a derisive grin on his countenance. For once he had gained the upper hand.

Mackenzie gulped like a fish and vanished through the wall.

6

Delighted with his gambit, the pop star tripped lightly over to the computer.

The screen showed Emerald sleeping none too comfortably in the chair at her patient's bedhead. From time to time her body twitched and she would mumble something.

A soft voice was reciting poetry at her: 'Awake, for morning in the bowl of night has flung the stone that puts the stars to flight… You know how little while we have to stay, and once departed may return no more…'

The voice became more insistent: 'Come on, you gorgeous creature, I've got a job for you. Awake! We have to get the Other Self out of the coma.'

The girl shifted in her sleep. She had a lovely dream. Bob Treillet was in the bed but he wasn't ill at all, he was just gazing at her with loving eyes. She went to the bed, tore back the sheet, to run her hands all over his torso until he drew her down on him and they exchanged a luscious kiss as his busy fingers sneaked under her hem, his bone hard phallus pressing into her abdomen. Melting into him, she began humming the tune of Death to My Other Half…

Bob meanwhile was striving to get a message through to her. The airwaves crackled, giving him feedback from the girl's dream. Shocked, he realized it wasn't him in the dream, but his Other Self!

'Ay-ay-ay,' he wailed. 'The bastard's at her again!'

He jumped as footsteps behind him told of Archie's reappearance. He was carrying a Greek urn.

This time, Archie had resolved to back Treillet, with or without Daisy's help. Even though his life had not been a model of success, at any rate his death need not be a complete waste of time.

'Leave that computer alone,' Mackenzie told him. 'Zior is changing the access code.'

'What's that weird jar you're carrying? You going in for pottery?'

'It was a hobby of mine at one time. I'm going to help you return to Earth, and I need this amphora, as it's correctly called.'

Bob was irritated in the extreme. 'For pity's sake make up your mind. You said a moment ago that it was impossible for me to go back.'

'If you hadn't tried to outsmart us, it would have been easier. There is still a remote chance,' Archie enthused. 'But it needs your full co-operation. This is how matters stand. As you know, the immortality formula calls for unshakeable faith, and without that you'll have real trouble getting through the tunnel. You have to vanquish those demons first.'

'Fair enough.'

'I am going to carry out two tests on you, to find out if you have the slightest chance of getting through. Correct me if I'm wrong, but I think you have a horror of snakes and similar creepy-crawlies.' Bob nodded a few times. 'That is what we call a phobia, and the best way of beating a phobia is to re-live your fear and overcome it.'

'So the shrinks claim. Yes, I hate snakes. When I was going through my driving test up a winding hill, a snake crossed the road and I skidded into a tree, almost plunging into a ravine. Naturally I failed the test.'

'What species of snake was it?' Archie asked him, waggling an arm to imitate a snake about to strike.

'A grass snake,' Bob said miserably.

'Good, so we'll start there. If you can overcome that phobia we'll move onto the second test, which concerns your horror of priests and organized religion generally. Don't forget that, if and when you return to Earth, you will join up with your body and will once again feel physical and mental sensations, good and bad.'

'Priests and religion, you say? I don't mind sacrificing myself for others, but changing my fundamental opinions is out of the question. Besides, having my poor body end up nailed on some cross isn't my cup of tea. A certain J.C. might see it as unfair competition on my part. You wouldn't want me to offend Him.'

'Daisy would never forgive us for that,' said Archie profering him the jar. 'We'll handle that subject later. For the present I want you to take this cobra out of the amphora.'

'A cobra! I told you it was a grass snake. This one is poisonous. You're not playing fair.'

'If you can beat it, you can beat any phobia about snakes. Go ahead, don't worry about the cobra biting you, up here we don't feel any pain, you know that. See, the snake is more scared than you are. Try and see if you can tame it. Cobras can be quite friendly if you treat them right.'

'I suppose next thing you'll want me to wear a false nose and make it laugh. How awful, the nasty slimy creature.'

'Don't be unkind to it, you haven't even seen it yet.'

There was no choice but to put his hand in the jar and get the damn thing out. He concentrated hard on the initials L-S-F in the hope that blind trust in the formula would see him through.

Archie was showing him what to do, slipping a couple of fingers past the neck of the jar, then pulling them back in double quick time. He showed a snake bite on one of his fingers.

'Crikey, it bit you,' cried Bob. 'If it attacks you, what chance have I got?'

'You should stop doubting all the time, simply shove your hand in and pull it out,' Archie told him, delighted in his role of mentor.

Bob took a deep breath, concentrated, and thrust his hand in.

'There's nothing there. It's empty!' he shouted, smashing the jar against the wall. 'You crafty begger, I bet you already had that bite on your finger. You just wanted to tell me I'd failed the test. You're no better than a rotten snake yourself.'

'That's what Daisy said,' Archie chortled. 'She reckons I'm the snake she harbours in her breast. Anyhow, it looks like you beat the first phobia, chummy. Now for the second. Take five, as we say in the profession; you can have five minutes' rest, I'm sure you need it.'

The success of this first test gave Bob a lift. He sidled over to the computer keyboard, intending to get through to his Other Self if he could. Down in the intensive care unit, he discovered a priest standing next to the bed. He recognized him from his schooldays, it was the detested prior at the college. The fellow began administering extreme unction to him, the sacrament supposed to help you into the after-life, alternatively to improve health.

Bob was disgusted by such 'provocation', as he deemed it. He regretted not getting even with the priest and his gang at school for all the cruelties they perpetrated. The prior was lucky he hadn't put white spirit into the communion wine as he meant to. The servant of God would have looked pretty silly breathing fire all over the altar. They'd have taken him off screaming, locked him up and garroted him for dealing with the Devil, just like they used to in the Middle Ages. And later if they'd have found out that it was all a prank, the bishop would have ordered the wretched prior to try to exorcise the boy. Bob would have preferred to deal with the Devil in order to see the last of the prior once and for all. The said prior would rather have killed himself than admit his own defeat. Then the Vatican would have excommunicated him. Alleluia! Treillet would finally have been delivered of their sanctimonious tyranny!

Bitterly, he regretted his failure to act. Sartre had declared that hell was other people, but Bob's hell was his Other Self constantly sapping his will.

Bob made a rude gesture to the priest standing next to the bed. The prior gave up, made a sign of the cross at Treillet, and disappeared.

* * *

When Dr. Koln sent Olga and Honorine away from the intensive care unit, they hung about in the corridor, where he subsequently gave them a further piece of his mind.

During the heated exchange they informed him that they had joined the Association for Dignified Death.

This item of news convinced him that they would make another attempt to send the patient into the next world.

It also gave him an idea. And the following day he contacted the girls again, telling them to pay a last visit to Treillet, as he was in the ultimate phase. Ethically, he couldn't cut off the oxygen supply, but they would be welcome to do it, he'd show them which tube to disconnect, he said.

He asked them to give him a few moments alone with the patient. He then deftly tampered with the equipment, fitting a second oxygen supply, which in reality was a dummy supply. That way, the real supply would be maintained, but the girls wouldn't know it.

The aim of his plan was to switch bodies. It would be a simple matter to obtain the corpse of an unidentified street junkie and label it 'Robert Treillet'. Meanwhile the real Treillet would be secretly transferred to another clinic with the Eurasian nurse, who would continue caring for him. The substitute corpse would be cremated and the girls would be none the wiser.

Olga and Honorine duly paid their visit to the intensive care unit, along with Bernard. Olga stood ready in the darkened room, the other two a few paces away, all looking grimly at Dr. Koln. The surgeon gave a brief nod and Olga turned off the dummy oxygen supply. The electrocardiogram, as modified by Koln, went flat and a reverent bush fell on the room. Only Koln and Emerald knew that Treillet was still breathing.

Bernard reflected that a proper funeral would have made a worthwhile event for the media, it would have made the 8p.m. news. They could have worked up some suitable epitaphs for the headstone, something like: 'To an immortal artist' or 'May the angels be your chorus' or 'Eternal rest grant him O Lord' – professional, romantic or standard variety to suit all tastes.

Bernard was not so much cynical as incapable of forgetting the public relations angle surrounding any event. He had used the media in Bob's interest, and vice versa. That was the way of the world and he was certainly not going to change the arrangements just to be different. They had all made an excellent team, the anarchistically inclined pop star modelling himself approximately on Bob Dylan and the late French anarchist singer Leo Ferré, drawn as he was to a Utopian ideal. They could have made the most of all that at the funeral.

Even so, Bernard felt uneasy that he had exploited Bob outrageously, turning a sincere performer into a marketable product. As Daisy might have said, in his own way he was Cain who had killed his brother Abel.

For the second test, concerning religion, Archie had donned his suit of tails. It was the exact replica of the outfit he would have worn on the opening night of Manhattan Follies, if his destiny had been to attend that great occasion. Lacking faith in the existence of any deity and purpose to Creation, Mackenzie readily evoked the hand of destiny to account for the injustices he suffered.

He used his cane to switch off the computer.

'We don't need that for the second test,' he said with a chuckle. 'I suppose these electronic devices are a better way of communicating than the old style post office. When I was in the army I wrote to a girl every day for three months. But I gave it up, she never replied. I found out later she'd run off with the postman.

'I guess now she would run off with a repair technician working for Internet.'

Archie assumed a serious expression.

'Zior has informed me that the Supreme Power is considering our future at this very moment. Not only Daisy's and mine, but yours too.'

'In that case we'd better put our skates on,' Bob said. 'I'm ready myself but we can't be sure that my Other Self will co-operate. It'll be his fault if there's a cock-up in the tunnel.'

Mackenzie had come to realize that this Other Self of Bob's was a separate being, rather than merely a figment of Bob's subconscious. In other words the Other Self was an independent entity. Archie had hoped that Treillet would simply ignore his Other Self, whereas during his stay at the Centre he had continued hating him more intensely.

'As I understand it, your Other Self is your opposite number. Am I right?'

'He's not in the same category as I am,' Bob replied. 'I want nothing to do with that depressing imbecile. All he does is sing the Passion according to Saint Jeremiad.'

'Let's forget the theology for the moment Let's agree that you yourself are the embodiment of thoughtlessness, while the Other Self is the incarnation of caution, so to speak. Since you yourself act according to your feelings, you must have the advantage over him and decidedly so.'

'I'll go along with that.'

'It's hard to say whether you've understood or whether you make out that you don't,' said Archie wagging his head. 'When you put your hand in the jar, you believed the cobra was inside. Now be honest, do you think your Other Self would have taken the risk?'

'Can't say.'

'Anyone as clued-up as the Other Self wouldn't take a chance like that. In the same way, anyone in a state of clinical death, as you are, doesn't imagine they will recover.'

'Ask Freud. Mind you, he too went a bit gaga himself in the end.'

'I'm only trying to sort you out. In this second test, we are trying to evaluate your human qualities in the light of your present mental condition. I am hoping for an intuitive reaction from you rather than a cerebral one. Up here, the heart takes precedence over reason, as you doubtless realize.'

Bob rubbed his chin. 'There doesn't seem to be much rhyme or reason up here. I have the distinct impression,

Archie, that you are about to involve me in another of your high wire acts, with me falling into the bucket of whitewash.'

'You must realize, Bob, if you plan one day to illuminate your fellow beings, I'd like to make sure that the immortality formula is in reliable hands. Even supposing that your project works out, I can't be certain the Supreme Power will forgive me for letting you loose down there.'

'I'm sure that with your subtle mind you'll be able to conjure up a few mitigating circumstances, if there's a flop.'

'Possibly, but the Supreme Power happens to be smarter than I am.'

Mackenzie was prepared to accept that the Supreme Power signified redemption, but he feared that his own interference in divine matters might lose him the deity's mercy for ever. He twitched his head irritably; this was no time to worry about redemption, mercy and the rest of Daisy's religious mumbo-jumbo. One thing was certain, Zior would call any bluff of his while he was listing his mitigating circumstances. He'd need to come up with something spectacular if he were to avoid the wrath of his superiors. He'd need a winning hand at that poker session, and no mistake. Already, a scheme was forming in his mind.

Manifestly, he calculated, Treillet had settled into his twin personality. Moreover, the fellow could be dangerous, he might appear to be an inspired prophet of some kind, but he could also turn out to be an inspired politician and that could lead to anything. When Treillet was back on Earth, there would be no controlling him, which meant that, before letting him go, Mackenzie had to be sure that Bob would operate hand-in-hand with this Other Self of his. The Other Self would calm him down and maybe give his project every scope for success. If the whole thing flopped, Treillet would have to fend for himself, while he, Archie, would need to go down on his knees and beg Zior's indulgence. As was well known, a fault admitted is a fault half pardoned. The only trouble was that it would remain half condemned!

Emerging from his ruminations, Archie said with a show of joviality: 'Now then, we've wasted enough time in useless talk.

All set for the second test?'

'If I have to have it, let's get started'

'I want you to improvise. Imagine you're in the woods gathering mushrooms.'

'Oh great. I'd trade a week in eternity any day for a fry-up of wild mushrooms and a decent red wine. A good old Pisse Dru would be perfect.'

Archie bounced his cane and caught it nimbly. 'So glad the idea puts you in a good humour, long may it last. Now suppose you hear some cries for help while you're scrabbling around for your dinner, and you go toward the cries, which are coming from an old lady tied to an oak tree. Her body has been lacerated with a knife of some sort. "Fear not, madam," you holler, "I am your knight in shining amour, etc., etc." Nearby you catch sight of a stack of timber with an axe leaning up against it. You grab the axe. But lo, from a thicket there leaps the lady's mad attacker and he starts cutting her up some more. What do you do? You have three seconds to reply starting now!'

'Well I...'

'Just tell me what you do, for Pete's sake,' Archie yelled.

Treillet gave a shrug.

'A maniac torturing a defenceless old lady has no right to live. If the lady is still more alive than dead, I would give her first aid. Otherwise, if she's too far gone I'd finish her off and put her out of her agony. As to her assailant I would chop him into mincemeat.'

Mackenzie shook his head. 'Thou shalt not kill. As Daisy would say, we don't have the same values.'

'With that kind of demented fool, there's no alternative. I would kill him.'

'How mean. What about forgiveness? Sorry, pal, I'd have given my all to get you back to Earth. As things are, I can only trust that you will learn wisdom in due course. Ask your Other Self about it.'

Without more ado, Archie danced out of the white-walled room.

* * *

Bob shook his fists at the sky, hot waves of anger welling up in his chest.

He began punching the computer in his rage, smashing the keyboard to smithereens. As the keys flew out, they reflected aspects of his past, furtive scenes from decades scattered with failures, regrets and misery.

His last hope of joining up with his body again had been dashed. He had no option now but to get on his knees and beseech his Other Self to join him at the Centre.

Precisely as he was about to do just that, a cloud appeared at the door of the room.

'Golly, that was quick,' he exclaimed. 'I hadn't even started praying. This is my Other Self. I know what I'll do, I shall propose a non-aggression pact, and put in a clause saying it is renewable every twelve months.'

His jaw dropped when he realized that the misty shape was turning into – John Warden, of all people!

'W-Where did you spring from?' Bob spluttered.

'That tunnel thing,' said the senator. 'Didn't think much of it, we build 'em better in the States. You speak French, I notice, so can I. My old dad was at one time U.S. ambassador in Paris and I picked up a few phrases as a boy.'

'B-But tell me, sir, how did you come to take that route. This is the Universal Selection Centre. We seem to be in the same predicament.'

'It was like this,' Warden drawled. 'I was doing a campaign tour and reached San Francisco where I gave a speech at Berkeley on the Third World population problem. Some crazy coot fired a couple of shots at me, and I can only suppose that I'm dead. You must be part of the welcome committee. Glad to meet you.'

Bob waved his hands in negation. 'No no no, you aren't dead. Take my advice and get out of here before they put you on their storage disks. They're all lunatics here. Go back at once.'

'Who's they?'

'Two clowns called Archie and Daisy. Now go!'

'Take it easy, I'm sure I'm dead. One of the bullets got me right here in the chest, straight through the heart, I guess.'

Bob waggled his head, Gallic style. 'You certainly take things calmly. But hurry, don't hang around.'

'You mean go back through the tunnel?'

'Yes, don't take any notice of the monsters.'

'What monsters? I didn't see any monsters.'

'No monsters?' said Bob, his agitation subsiding.

'Nope, not even the smell of one.'

'In that case,' Bob said, 'You must have excellent protection, close surveillance of some kind.' Treillet eyed him narrowly and took his arm. 'I wonder if I might come a little way with you. I was planning to go back through the tunnel myself, as it happens.'

Bob deduced that, since the new voyager had reached the Centre without incident, he must have some charmed quality that staved off any forces of Evil. He was therefore a person well worth cultivating. The idea of rubbing shoulders again with human beings occasioned him an instant of apprehension, but the newcomer looked to be his final opportunity to return earthwards and carry out his planetary mission. If he missed his chance, even Archie would never forgive him.

'Excuse me asking,' Warden was saying, 'but who are you exactly? What's upset you here? Where's God? I'd like a word with Him.'

'My name is nobody. I don't know anyone called God. There's just Archie and Daisy and someone called Zior whom no-one ever sees.'

'Sounds fishy to me. My name is Warden, John Warden.'

'I know about you. You're the presidential candidate with the big reform policy. But the conservatives are fighting it. I like your ideas, they're different from that old change-with-continuity stuff. Even so, your plan for I.Q. testing to stop half-wits breeding like rabbits could lead to big problems. Let's hope there'll be someone left to have children.'

Warden chuckled and slapped his thigh. 'The present so-called System tends to breed sheep and lemmings. I agree that my plan runs counter to it, but someone has to put a stop to the rot.'

'Better to change the System, surely. Perhaps the chap who fired at you was from the sheep and lemmings.'

'So you think it was organized?'

'Bet my bottom dollar it was.'

'I'd say he was just some mental defective.'

'There must be scores of lobbies out to get you.' Treillet said evenly. 'One of them had a contract out against you. Remember the Kennedy saga.'

'You could be right. My daughter warned me against running for president. I should have listened.'

Bob kept looking round to make sure Archie and Daisy were not putting in another appearance.

'Come on, John,' he urged. 'Let's go. By the way, my name's Bob Treillet.'

7

They were half way through the tunnel when Bob skidded to a halt. He fancied he heard worrying noises. Gritting his teeth, thinking L-S-F, L-S-F, L-S-F, he moved hesitantly ahead once more, with Warden in front of him.

'Keep going, I'm right behind you,' he urged.

'So I notice. If you want a leader, I'm your man.'

'John,' Bob ventured. 'I'd like to tell you something. When we're through the tunnel we shall separate, but I want to say that, while I admire your courage, I suspect that your programme is too advanced for most people. You have to play them along, don't rush your fences because it rarely works. I know from my own sad experience. Be smart, stick to your objectives and you'll win through.'

'Well thanks, Bob. Sounds like good advice, I'll bear it in mind.'

'Play it like your rivals for the White House, promise the moon and the public will back you.'

'If I were a Britisher, I'd say I always play a straight bat. The voters know that I do. By the way, what's all this L-S-F patter you're handing out? Ever since we got into the tunnel, you keep mumbling L-S-F.'

'It's too long a story, I'll explain it some time. Keep going, we're doing fine,' Bob ordered.

Warden turned and took a long look at his travelling companion.

'Next month,' he said, 'I'm throwing a garden party for my

daughter. She'll be twenty. I'd be mighty glad if you could join us. Where do I have the invitation sent?'

'Poste restante, 83990, Saint-Tropez, France.'

As Bob spelled out the address, the full realization of his journey home to France overwhelmed him. His heart gave a leap when he registered the amazing fact that they had outwitted Archie and Daisy. An immense desire to live bore his astral body along. Once again he would see the glorious Mediterranean seaboard, once again he would hear the lazy brogue of the South as he shared a ratatouille or an aioli with a friend and they sank a bottle of Côte de Provence rosé with its keen earthy tang and looked out on the azure blue under a cloudless sky. Prior, of course, to working out the details of his epoch-making project. He felt heady already; if his Other Self were unwilling to join him, he would darn well join his Other Self whether he liked it or not. And would master him.

As they neared the Earth end of the tunnel a loud siren wail assailed his ears. Gathering all his strength, he prepared for the last stage of the journey.

Elated beyond measure, he shot out of the gloom via a trapdoor. The trap slammed behind him with a clatter, but his tunic was caught in it. Tugging fiercely, he heard it rip. He abandoned it and leapt forward.

He was back on Earth!!! And Warden was nowhere to be seen.

Bob Treillet, lying in the clinic where Koln had transferred him, began moving.

Opening his eyes, he cautiously scanned what he could see of the room. He knew he was in a bed, and tried a few small motions with his arms and legs, then turned his head this way and that. Slowly he pushed down his arms, and finally sat up completely. He pinched himself, digging his now-sharp nails into his forearm.

Bob cried out with the pain. He was alive and kicking!!!

It took Treillet perhaps half a minute to comprehend that he was emerging from a coma. The first and, he hoped, the last coma he would ever experience this side of the grave.

He frowned, aware that he had travelled, he had been elsewhere in the interim. How long had he been in the coma? Woozily, the voyage to the Centre, his anguished stay there and his triumphant return – all this came back to him. He had gone through a genuine near-death saga and, by jimminy, was he glad it was over! He had been privileged to gain a glimpse of the hereafter, and no scientist or doctor or psychiatrist, however eminent, would be able to explain that.

A mental image of Archie and Daisy flashed through his mind and his stomach gave a momentary lurch. He felt sick and lay back again, dismissing the picture with difficulty.

He addressed his Other Self, suggesting that they forget the past, let bygones be bygones, and unite their energies to set up the Union for Renovating the Planet.

His Other Self listened to Bob's truncated account of the adventure 'up there', more than once bursting into scornful laughter.

'We'll see who laughs last,' Bob chided.

Oddly, the Other Self began cringing in fright.

'Nom d'un chien!' Bob choked.

There was a flash of lightning. Mackenzie and Lady Sniffington-Madley were standing at the foot of the bed.

Treillet instantly closed his eyes in disbelief, then gradually opened them again. Oh no! They were still there!

'Cuckoo, it's us again,' chirped Archie, throwing Bob's ripped tunic on the coverlet.

'They're real,' the Other Self breathed. 'They are like you said.'

Bob hastened to remind his Other Self that this was no time to break down, but on the contrary they should react in unison. Get ready to fight for their lives.

Mackenzie, still with his cane, was wearing a navy blue suit with gold epaulettes on the jacket and a red stripe down each trouser leg; he looked like a jazzed up version of a Salvation Army official. Daisy wore a black alb and veil.

Archie brandished his cane and seemed on the point of laying into Bob with it.

'Don't worry, Monsieur Treillet,' Daisy said. 'We haven't come to get you.'

'Zior instructed us to chaperon you,' Archie explained. 'The powers-that-be decided that I'd been dishonest with you, and that it wasn't fair on you. They concluded that you should be given another chance. It's the luck of the Devil, I'd say.'

'Pity the trapdoor didn't finish you off.'

'Unfortunately,' Daisy said, ignoring the remark, 'we couldn't catch up with you. The result is that, instead of elevating ourselves, we have come down with a bump.'

'Another result, I suppose, is that I shall have to drag you around with me for the rest of my life.'

There was a brief silence and Archie observed: 'It didn't take you long to come to your senses down here.'

'We shan't be a nuisance,' her ladyship told Treillet in her high-faluting tone. 'You alone will be able to see us, and we'll try not to be an embarrassment to you. Incidentally, we should love to know who it was who helped you back through the tunnel. Tell us that and we shall leave you in peace, if you're nice to us. You can't make us believe you made the journey all on your own, I don't believe that for a moment.'

'I received some assistance,' Bob replied snootily.

'Who was it? Stop prevaricating.'

'His Other Self, I guess,' Archie snorted. 'It must have been him, but we'll deal with Mister Double-Cross later.'

Daisy leaned ominously over the bed: 'I must tell you this, Monsieur Treillet, we have been posted here against our wishes. I can also say that, in spite of our little differences in the past, Archie and I have made it up and we're quite love-birds now.' She took Archie's hand. 'We should have preferred to continue our ascension to higher spiritual planes rather than start again from scratch. All we ask of you now is a reasonable attitude, you must forget your search for immortality and give up your absurdly presumptuous idea for a Union for Renovating the Planet. As of now, I command you to forget your Other Self. We had enough bother from you without having the Other on our backs. I hope this is clear.'

'As always you are direct and crystalline.'

This seemed to satisfy Daisy for the moment. Bob eased himself out of the bed and stood beside it. He detached the drip-feed from his arm.

'You're not thinking of going some place?' Archie rapped, moving to the window.

'There's a friend I'd like to ...'

His Other Self cut him short, advising him to divulge nothing, otherwise his uninvited guests were sure to dupe him in some way. Bob would do better to find a quick route to San Francisco, where John Warden was currently in the hospital. It was imperative that Archie and Daisy should lose track of Bob Treillet for good, and calling on Warden was likely to achieve that, his alter ego stressed.

'Who is this friend?' Daisy demanded, Gestapo style.

'Er, the chaplain allotted to me at school,' Bob lied. 'You know, the college where I enjoyed a brilliant but miserable education that led nowhere. Thank goodness my real education started when I left school. To change the subject, it's the weekend and it gives me an idea. Tomorrow is Sunday, Daisy, and I wouldn't miss you if you wanted to take a trip to London. I expect you'd like to see Buckingham Palace again. Incidentally, it's open to the public but no doubt they'd let you in for nothing.'

'The public!' Daisy exclaimed. 'Whatever next! All those sweaty working people in the royal chambers eating crisps out of a bag, urchins with dirty knickers running about the place. Oh my beloved country, that it should come to this. Is nothing sacred anymore?'

'The Queen's short of cash, apparently.'

'Even so! I must see about this,' her ladyship trumpeted. She seemed ready to swim the Channel in order to put things right.

Bob turned to her companion: 'In your case, Archie, I warmly suggest that you get yourself a seat on Concorde – that masterpiece of French technology – and take a look at the Big Apple. I'm sure you'd like to see how *Manhattan Follies* is faring. Think of that billboard I told you about. What an insult. If I were you I'd start proceedings against that Zbigeskwirtski chap. Don't take it lying down, old fellow.'

Archie looked ready to take a space rocket rather than Concorde to get his revenge.

Treillet casually picked up the torn tunic that Mackenzie had saved from the tunnel trapdoor. He put it on over his hospital blouse.

'If I wear this, you won't lose sight of me,' he assured them. 'I could hardly be more co-operative, don't you agree? Well then, I wish you both a pleasant weekend. Let's meet up for breakfast on Monday at my place. Do you take tea or coffee?'

'No need to play hide-and-seek with us,' Daisy chided. 'Zior's orders were clear, we must not lose sight of you for a single instant.'

Bob gave a chuckle. He began making a theatrical bow to signal his departure, but accidentally tore a plasma bag on a hook over the bed. The contents spattered over his tunic.

Immediately, an electric sign over the door showed the three figures 666, Satan's very own number.

Archie glanced at the number without realizing its significance. Daisy went as white as a sheet and began reciting the Litany from the Book of Common Prayer.

The door from the corridor opened briskly and Emerald the Eurasian nurse hurried in with a trayful of pills, to see Treillet, his white tunic stained with blood and his arms outstretched as if in benediction.

'Jesus Christ!' she yelled.

'Emerald!' he yelled back.

The girl released a groan, dropped the tray with a deafening clatter, and swooned into Bob's arms.

He lifted her up and laid her on the bed.

Daisy, her eyes fixed on the electric sign, choked: 'It's horrible, I think I'm going to be sick.'

'Probably you're feeling earthsick,' Bob jested. 'Unless it's a sign of extraterrestrial pregnancy. They've got a gynaecology department here, I've no doubt. If it's triplets, Daisy, don't forget to put one by for me.'

'Don't be ridiculous,' she told him. 'Medical science can do nothing for me, as you well know.'

Archie meanwhile took the nurse's pulse and examined the whites of her eyes.

'Traumatic blackout, get a doctor!'

Treillet grabbed a bulb-shaped emergency knob, but it came away in his hand. He glared at Archie.

'Don't glare at me with those murderous eyes.' Mackenzie said. 'It ain't my fault, Daisy's neither. Could be Zior up to a few games.'

'Archie, if you're still thinking of keeping me in your clutches, forget it,' Bob warned him. 'I'm free again, and if you play any of your games, like taking Emerald as a hostage, I'll make you pay for it for the rest of eternity.'

Mackenzie gave him a quick smile. 'Talking of eternity, if I were you I wouldn't hang around here any longer. The kind of miraculous cure you've had doesn't occur every day. You must realize that once those doctors know what's happened they'll never let you go. They will even exhibit you like a circus animal. From the legal standpoint you're dead and about to be cremated. You can't come back to life.'

Treillet stood motionless and open-mouthed. That's terrific, it dawned on him. What a wonderful opportunity! Dead to all intents and purposes, he was incognito, the invisible man made flesh. He could start all over again, living a completely new existence as someone else if he liked. With everything he'd learned during his flight to the Centre and back, he could avoid all those annoying mistakes he'd made in the past. And to crown it all, he possessed the immortality formula, which he could summon up whenever he felt the need. This new turn of events changed everything!

Archie was opening the window, looking out into the black night.

'You're in luck, they've got you on the ground floor, and it's on the garden side. Hm, smells like Provence herbs.'

He made a show of sneezing a couple of times.

'Curses, it's the pollen, an allergy I've had since childhood,' Archie complained.

'Good gracious,' Bob exclaimed, 'Has your sense of smell returned?'

'Of course not, but I have a vivid imagination. Your country is like Italy, what dreams are made of.'

The resurrected songster took a last look at Emerald. 'So far I've watched her only on the computer screen. Now I can see that she is a thousand times more beautiful in reality. When she comes round, tell her I love her, that I'll get in touch with her, that I'll find a way of curing her leukaemia.'

'Quick,' Archie said in a stage whisper. 'Someone's coming along the passage.'

Daisy wrested her gaze from the figures 666, to see Bob clambering out of the window. She brandished her prayer book at him.

The born-again Treillet leapt out into the darkness.

Bob Treillet plunged like a ton of bricks from the tenth floor of the clinic.

'I'll get you for this!' he bellowed in a dramatic diminuendo, as Mackenzie doubled over in uncontrollable mirth.

Archie left the window and told Daisy. 'He always leaps before he looks. But he nearly ruined everything with his infatuation for this young lady here. Zior would have never forgiven us for failing our mission. I knew he would act impulsively, my little ploy was foolproof. From Mackenzie to macadam! It was a cast iron scheme. This time they'll scoop him up with a shovel. This time we've foiled him.'

He celebrated his victory with a tap dance, flinging his cane up and catching it adroitly. He ended the performance on one knee, arms extended to receive the plaudits of a make-believe public.

'Stop messing about and get ready to receive his soul as it comes up.' Daisy ordered.

'You're right darling. There's not a second to lose. Zior gave us fifteen minutes, remember, to take his soul back up. Daisy, for the love of Mike, quit sermonizing. Gimme that thing!'

He wrenched the prayer book from her hands and hurled it out through the window.

'Archie, that's sacrilege,' she screamed. 'Do you know what those figures 666 mean over the door?'

'Nope. Never was any good at figures. OK, what the hell does it mean?'

'It's the Devil's own number. Holy cats, Satan is among us.'

'Sure He is, this is Planet Earth, He's everywhere. Pull yourself together, the minutes are ticking by. Gimme a hand here.'

The pair leaned out of the window, as the nurse stirred on the bed. 'I love you,' she moaned.

'Get ready for hauling-in,' Archie crowed. 'What goes down must come up.'

A three-ton open truck sped away from the building, heading for the street exit. It was loaded to the brim with bulky bags of laundry, on the top of which a man was struggling to keep his balance.

'Dammit,' said Archie, 'That's Treillet. He's getting away!'

Bob was sitting on the load, roaring his head off. He waved goodbye to them and made an impolite gesture in their direction with his arm.

The emissaries from the Centre shut the window with a bang. They stared at each other, only to realize that their plastic bodies were undergoing a change. The material seemed to be bubbling and it started to split open in places.

Daisy's eyes popped as Archie's jacket swelled up, two round bumps developing on his chest. At the same time her own bosom was deflating. Their hands went down and they found that their genitalia were changing too.

'I'm a woman and you're a man!' Archie squawked in a soprano voice. 'This is Zior's doing. He's punishing us because we lost Treillet.'

'Oh Lord, this is the end,' Daisy boomed out in a rich baritone.

Swaying with the rolling motion of the truck, Bob clutched a couple of laundry bags, asking his Other Self to help him exterminate Zior's agents.

His Other Self, in his down-to-earth way, remarked that it was only by the merest stroke of luck that they had managed to escape on the truck. Daisy, he reminded Bob, believed him to be an acolyte of Lucifer and would move Heaven and Earth to catch him. The Sniffington-Madleys of this world always won in the end and it was hardly worth trying to flee.

'Rubbish,' Bob scoffed. 'We've done pretty well so far. Who dares wins.'

Treillet began softly humming a new song, dedicated to human advancement.

His Other Self reluctantly agreed it had possibilities. He even went so far as to hazard a title for it: Let's Dream As One.